Everything Must Go

Presented To:

____

By:

____

On:

____

Books by Greg Luti

Collected Poems

Everything Must Go

Everything Must Go

3

Everything Must Go

Greg Luti

gregluti.com

ISBN – 978-1-7340110-3-6

Edited by Greg Luti

Cover Design by Greg Luti

Cover Art by German Creative

Preface

I wrote these stories over the course of about ten years or so. Some of them are from as recent as only a few years ago, while others are from my earlier college days. I decided to finally get them all together and put them all into one collection. I included a few from my blog, Pens and Words, as I felt that would make this collection better.

As for the topic of these short stories, they are all over the place. I drew inspiration from the various parts of my life, from the jobs that I had, to the people that I knew then. I credit them for the variety as much as some skill on my end.

The title of the book came from a Facebook reader suggesting it.

The book cover came from me, and I originally gave it to my book cover artist black and white and she added the red to it.

I hope that the reader can find a few of these stories charming and worth reading, as I do with other short stories.

Greg Luti – Friday – 6/21/24

Everything Must Go

Table of Contents

Everything Must Go

Everything Must Go

Transfer from NIR

Transfer From NIR

Please don't be mistaken by my casual demeanor or nonchalant attitude, for I had a good reason to ask for a transfer out of the park where I worked for a little less than eight months. That I did, do not be surprised if my request is not the last you will hear of a disgruntled worker. Now I won't stand before you and act as though I am a well thought individual with a reason behind each thing I do. Educated, yes, with the ability to claim an upbringing of books and schooling. But prepared? Most certainly not. This reason for my departure, I am confident, is one of my more sound decisions. Ironically enough, it has to do with insanity.

The most obvious and blatant is that my boss Douglas Beil, the man in charge of Ned Irving Redding Park, NIR for short, is, in fact, a madman. Half-brother twice removed to the Prince of Darkness. In a previous life, he ate at the same dining table as Dracula in hell and toasted to the mayhem they spread across the land, more proud of their hands of destruction than any word of accidental cruelty they witnessed. As if he knew only how to be confrontational and uneasy with every person he met. There was nothing calm in his bones. No place for a heart. No way for a heart to even be put. In each situation, he had to show you that he was better than you. Never could anyone win a verbal argument with the man. I won't even mention physical battles here since he lacked much in that area. He spoke of playing hockey in the past, but I never bought it. He almost tripped whenever he walked, and he expected me to believe he could skate. Yeah right. An athlete was something Doug Beil was not. However, he would say differently, like many liars do.

He stood up not for truth like we learn in school was the cause of Socrates questioning the townspeople. No, he argued to let all know he was the smartest man in the room. No one ever believed it was him anyway. Not to toot my own horn, but I felt I possessed this title since I had the most schooling of the group, and when spoken to, I was clearly the most literate and intelligible of them. The smartest thing I did was not engage Doug in an argument.

Don't bother with idiots who think they are always right. Remember, they are idiots for a reason. That was my thinking, and it worked for the most part.

Despite having little knowledge of the maintenance job assigned to me, I worked mostly in customer service before this; I proved I could easily be taught and remember a task with no problem. Even Jimmy, the second in command, commented that I was a quick learner. If Doug did anything when he was trying to act smart, it was that he proved he was quite an idiot and would gladly embarrass someone just to make a point. I know this from firsthand experience since I read a book titled "Interesting Facts About History" during breakfast, and Doug made mean remarks about such a piece of literature, like I should be insulted for deciding to read rather than engage him in conversation.

Over time my boss's temperament got to all of his workers, especially, as I said since the guy had breakfast and lunch with them. Just thinking of it makes me shake my head in disgust. Eventually, all workers would leave and be replaced by other oblivious fools, leaving only two constant staff members, Doug, whom I feel I have described to the point where you understand his madness, and Jimmy. The two are so close to each other that they could be gay lovers if I didn't know they were married. I swear they act more like a couple than they do with their own wives. I can say this with confidence (at least for Doug's sake since his wife works in the same park, and I have seen them go back and forth.) Although the coworkers knew this of Doug and Jimmy, no one said anything. Because we didn't want to be buried in the back of the park. You think I am kidding or exaggerating. I'm not. Fear was a tool they used often. The threat of getting fired or sent home for the day was said as much as hello and goodbye. Also, Jimmy has a history of kind of losing it. One story was that he put a pitchfork to a patron's throat for not picking up some trash. Yeah, you try telling a guy with that type of anger that he is gay and tell me how it goes.

Despite all of this, my boss, the very man I hated, actually liked me. Yes, it is true. He appreciated the job I did for him. Which wasn't very much, I admit. Clean a bathroom here. Mop up a room there. Throw out the garbage when asked. Simple labor is more time-consuming than difficult. Unfortunately, these views only went on one way. Like all the workers before me, I immediately requested a transfer. What took them so long to get me out of NIR is a question I guess I will have to ask at a later date.

The last bit of news I heard before I left NIR is that Charles Helden, who everyone calls Helden, was suing Doug for taping a conversation they had, and without Helden's knowing, Doug went to the park's attorney to get him fired for what Helden said. I don't know what he actually said, but knowing Helden, it was probably a different opinion than Doug's. Helden is such a character who would not go along with Doug's nutty ways. Often telling me that Doug and Jimmy would work me til death to get the job done, so I should pace myself when gives a job since they will only reward me with more work. Such is the case with some bosses who unfortunately forget what it is like to be the lowest man on the totem pole. As soon as they get an office with a computer, they forget how to clean up and throw out the trash, and when asked if there is anything you can do to help them work, they give the chilling warning that "there is always something to do." This is another way of saying, "I'll make up stuff for you to do if I have to." Helden had a clever philosophy towards his job that he'd repeat to all who would listen "Work smarter, not harder." By that, he meant an intelligent approach that was easy on you is better than a stupid approach that would make you exhausted. He'd repeat this phrase as much as the bosses would threaten us, and he was quite proud of the originality of it, or at least from what we all knew, the phrase was credited to Helden and not stolen from another person. The attorney, of course, said the recording was foul play on Doug's part. *Self-incrimination. I plead the Fifth.* These terms were unknown to Doug, or he is just that big of an asshole. It could be both. You can't record someone without them knowing and then get them in trouble for it. Instead of directly bringing up the legal case at the new park, I waited for another coworker to ask me about my experience at NIR, hoping they play the role of the storyteller and not me. No one in the other parks like Doug, so gossip is already well-known. The employees often find themselves speaking of the others that have worked there. Where did the other worker go, and why did they leave? Do they work next week? Who is working with me? Common questions for a job that requires much interaction with others, naturally, we spoke of each other. In fact, the gay rumor stemmed from these types of talks, where one would whisper the news they heard because many believed Doug was too friendly with the teenage boys who work for him. Before I started working there, a young man is said to have gone everywhere with Doug to the point that it made others uncomfortable, for they only knew the young man through his alleged affair with the boss. It has been years since he left the job, and he came back to go around the park with his now wife and kids, and some of the coworkers could not believe he was who he claimed to be.

The first man I saw was Frank. He is in charge of the maintenance for the park I am at now and has been on the job for twenty-three years and means well. So he has the same authority as Doug but a bigger heart and more respect for his peers.

I spoke little ill words to him of my old boss, for I feel I gain nothing by doing such an act. I could have easily gone on a rant about Doug's madness, but it was not worth it in my eyes. When Frank asked me how it was working there (he knows of Doug's craziness), I pleasantly nodded and told him I was happy to be transferred.

"You got out of there right in time. That place is getting bad. Real bad." Frank told me in a serious tone. I had an idea of what he meant, but I wanted it to come from him, not me.

"What do you mean?" I asked, caught off guard. (but not really)

"The guy, Jimmy, over there, is suing Doug for listening in on a conversation the two had. Guy's taking everything that he can from Doug."

"You mean Helden, right?" I tried to confirm my sources since I had Helden in the legal case, not Jimmy.

"No, Jimmy." Frank corrected me. "It's bad over there. You got out just in time." He commented in his raspy voice as he leaned against the front desk, covering up the flyers about the next week's park events.

That guy is suing my former boss? Yes. That guy. The guy who was the only friend of the crazy boss I had, the man who sang with him at the piano in the main room to pass the time, who bought him breakfast and lunch, who he trusted him (on the outside) more than any other worker is going to get him fired. And is willing to go against him in a court of law to protect himself.

So as to your question, did I have a good reason for leaving NIR?

Yes. I say I did.

Television in the Hallway

Television in the Hallway

Mary needs her coffee in the morning; without it, she is a wreck, like she can't function in the morning wreck. It's the kind of wreck that makes you understand why so many people need coffee to even function. When you hear about a wreck on the news, surely one of them must be Mary in the mornings; she does not have her coffee. Alas, the reports are never that, and only minor incidents like car accidents.

Everything Must Go

This morning, she has to have some, or her physical education classes won't go smoothly. One student acted up yesterday, and Mary has to call his mother later today and report the foul language the first grader used. Billy called Janet stupid when they were playing kickball, and although Mary (Mrs. Ligil to the kids) warned Billy to stop, he continued. Mrs. Ligil had to tell Bill's homeroom teacher of the incident, and she informed her that she was going to have to call the boy's mother about this incident. Gym teachers can teach the kids everything about physical fitness, and yet, somehow, the kids always find a way to insult each other.

With her eyes barely open and her body still recovering from last night's karate class, she got out of bed to enjoy the best part of her day. Concerning her aches, she started to take some classes at a place in town. Not to defend herself from the awkward slackers she deals with on a daily basis, although she probably could (those kids can be a handful), but to keep her mature body in shape. The class she has is a hybrid of working out and learning a few self-defense moves. For the first half hour, the class of ten people is instructed to do pushups, situps, and other various full-body exercises that can help anybody trying to get fit and then each individual brings out the punching bag and takes a few swings, which is a sight to see I'm sure. The room is of middle-aged to senior-aged women, with not much power behind any of their punches.

From the hallway outside of Mary's room, a loud crash is heard, followed by, "Goddamnit!" Bob, Mary's husband, jammed his toe against the television in the hallway. Unlike most televisions, this one is not meant to be watched because it is broken. Although I am sure, there are some who would try doing that with the broken device, seeing the destruction as an opportunity for their ingenuity rather than a run to the garbage. For the majority of sane folks, the TV doesn't work. That is also the reason for its odd location in the house, rather than the conventional spot of a living room wall. It is large enough that when it collides with a half-asleep Bob in the unlit hallway, it wins. The only good part of the television was its durability. It lasted for seven years, and despite not being functional, it is still doing better than Bob's toe.

Cursing to himself, Bob stumbled back to bed, complaining of the injury the television caused. What can he do then but walk back in defeat? He can't yell at the TV, since it won't respond (being a TV and all), and he can't strike it back, for unlike a human, the TV can withstand hits from Bob. This inanimate object that had no strike ability or even a good right jab punch somehow beat Bob in a fight, and it was a loss he had to accept.

Without turning on any lights, Mary walked through the hallway until a noise made a little earlier was heard again, louder than before and also followed by "Goddamnit" For the record, Mary and Bob go to church on a limited basis only gathering for the Lord on Christmas and Ash Wednesday, seeing their weekend obligations as more pressing than the praise of the Savior. As long as there is no television around, they're fine.

Holding her left hip, Mary went back to the bedroom to tell Bob what happened.

"The damn TV." She notified the other injured party. No more had to be said as they lay in bed with their hands on their hips, and the grimaces on their faces said it all. They were hurt. And it was way too early to deal with it. One never likes to get injured, but one really hates injuries that occur alongside tiredness.

"We got to move that damn thing," Mary told Bob. What she really meant was that he should move it.

Knowing the true nature of the question, Bob answered. "I can't. I'm injured."

A roll of Mary's eyes wet unseen but felt by Bob, whose timid approach annoyed her and whose slick commands didn't sick well with him.

"Plus, it's too dark right now." He finished whatever meaningless defense he could muster.

He will never move that TV unless I tell him. What is wrong with him?

She doesn't see that I am hurt and that I can't move anything right now. What is wrong with her? Who the hell leaves a television in the middle of the hallway?

What is wrong with them?

They are injured.

The two lay there in bed for the next fifteen minutes, trying to recover, and talked about their day's events. Bob has an office meeting about inventory control. He tried to get a correct number the last time they had inventory, which always seemed too soon, but there seemed to be a problem. Somehow, the numbers are never what they should be. Even after thorough checks, recounts, and reports, somehow, the system gets broken, and someone in the office is left walking around cluelessly. "Why don't we have these? I thought we had these. I checked inventory, and it said we had them." Inventory is always right until you don't have any of the items you need. Then it is wrong. The person who complains about the items counted in inventory is never the person doing the actual counting.

Mary has to call a parent about a student's disruptive behavior, which I have already mentioned. She has experience with this, as the language of children is more advanced than their athletic ability, and learned a matter-of-fact indifference towards the person is the best way to handle it. Sure, the kid can't throw a ball, but he sure knows how to curse. Posing emotion never allows Mary to get to through the problem with the parent, as the parent is always ready to defend their child as if they are the golden child.

Both days went as well as they could go for each other. The inventory went smoothly, so in about a week from now, someone will complain about it. That's pretty good. Last year, someone complained by the end of the same day. And Billy's mom agreed to try to discipline her kid better. Until he does this same thing in the next class because his mom doesn't reinforce positive behavior with the kid. Not much got done, but progress was still made.

The next morning, Bob got up first, like he does most mornings, not that much earlier than Mary, but enough for him to settle himself at the kitchen table and have the pot on by the time she awoke.

Bob put his Ironman watch on his left wrist and got out of bed at a rate his frail body could handle. He opened the bedroom door to the hallway and slowly closed it behind him, not to wake his wife.

As if on cue, a loud bang was heard from the hallway, followed by the same phrase as yesterday. Mary called out to the victim of the crash, "Are you okay?"

Pissed at the unfortunate event, Bob told his wife, "I'll be at the computer."

Instead of going back to bed, he somehow stumbled his way to the computer table in the living room to read up on the latest news.

Mary woke up a little later and did not hit the television like her husband. The light from the morning sun made it visible. The worst part for her was that Bob forgot to put on the coffee.

Their follies of the past two days made for a great dinner conversation with their children, Steven and Naomi. Steve only heard what I wrote so far at the dinner table because he slept downstairs and in no way could hear any of the crashes and curses. Naomi, on the other hand, heard it all because her room was right next to the television that was hers before it broke. She heard the commotion of her parents but was too tired to react to it.

A month ago, the television went bad, and Naomi asked Bob to move it out of her room. Not having Steve around and getting no help from Naomi, Bob struggled to lift the television until he positioned it against the wall in the hallway and left it there. His exhaustion controlled his decision-making more than the reasonable place for the broken device. Little did he know of the pain he would experience by trying to save some of his energy.

After two morning injuries, Bob decided to listen to Mary and moved the television as soon as he got home from work. He dragged it into the living room, where it would be out of the way. Steve was nowhere to be found, so Bob was once again left to move the heavy television on his own. That is actually the same amount of help he got from his co-workers at the office meeting. The inventory is still a mess. But that is neither here nor there.

Later that night, when Mary got home from an after-school program, about, of all things, new ways that kids bully each other, the two went to a party of some friends they hadn't seen in a while. The relationship isn't what it used to be since it relied heavily on Steve's participation in sports, which is not around. That is, if sleeping isn't considered a sport. Mary and Bob's relationship with Steve's former friends took a turn for the worse when they found out that the same couples that attended Steve's games, who cheered from the stands, were also swingers. Being of Catholic faith, that idea terrified and disgusted the couple, who had been true to each other since the day they met. Up until that night, they only knew of swinging in a baseball context. All of the friends that they had known for the past ten years were now questionable characters in their eyes. Did they all do this? Did they do this while the kids grew up? Why did they only learn of this now? Answers that will remain a mystery to the reader

For my own sake (and for the reader), I will not go into details of the exchange of the previous night. All you need to know is that the couple was put into an uncomfortable and left shortly after.

That night, Naomi was also out at a party. Her friends didn't say anything strange or revealing to her. They just kept drinking at every bar they came across until the alcohol won, and a cab was needed as the only reliable means of transport.

That left Steve home for the night. All he did in his busy schedule was sleep and watch TV. Sometimes, at the same time, in order to really get work done. In between his 200th and 300th nap, he got off his but to get a snack that he didn't really need to eat. Was he that hungry? Not really. Was he starving? No. Could he still eat? Of course. On his way to the fridge, he saw the small desk that his sister had asked him to move upstairs. She was going to use it for makeup, eyeliners, and mirrors rather than sell it at a garage sale. Not wanting to intrude on his sister's room, he left the desk by the wall in the hallway.

Both parties ended late, and by the time both got home, Naomi was getting sober. Her parents were offended, and neither noticed Steve's move. His parents did notice that he left the television screen on and that the dishes were not done.

The next morning, Mary and Bob woke up earlier than the day before and discussed the unusual revelation of the last night. Neither of them were happy about it.

Mary got out of bed first and asked Bob if he wanted any coffee. She needed it. He is a tea person.

She opened the door and headed for the kitchen, leaving her husband thinking about the newly learned secret.

Within a few moments, an unfamiliar bang came from the hallway. The only distinguishable part was the remark shouted by Mary. "Goddamnit!"

Bob rushed to see what happened since he was well aware that he moved the television last night, and there was no reason why his wife should have walked into it.

Mary sat on the floor holding her hip, which will no longer be used for karate. "I thought you were going to move it."

Bob explained, "I did. Last night. Before the party."

He helped her gather herself as the two seniors struggled with maintaining their balances. Just as Mary got up on her feet, Naomi left her bedroom to go to the bathroom. "Oh look, Steve brought up my desk."

My Uncle Hilbert

My Uncle Hilbert

I begin this as a recollection of a man I knew very little about. The only person I can say who lived once but died twice, for we all live but one life on this Earth, learn what we can from the education system, make whatever money we can scourge up from our jobs, and die, leaving an end to the learning and the income. No mortal man dies twice. Unless, of course, one isn't talking about his physical body. What I learned of the man whose name this story bears I obtained through conversations with relatives, ease droppings at family gatherings, and stories from my parents I've heard my short while on this Earth. He was Uncle Hilbert to me, as I, like many, called him by the title out of respect for his sister, my mother, more than the man himself. Like aunt, the title uncle is unique to the individual for it signifies their place in the family, but the title is also used by many other families across the world. It is a fleeting title for one to have, for it is given to so many. I, along with the other nieces and nephews, called him Uncle Hilbert, and that soon led to some sort of characterization of his being. He was not just uncle, not just Hilbert, he was Uncle Hilbert. The uncle you wanted to avoid. The mean uncle. The weird uncle. The uncle no one liked. To the coroner's office, he was Hilbert Gadley, of 92 years, weighed 143 pounds, and had a height of 5 feet and 2 inches. He had brown eyes, and his cause of death was that of natural causes. I'm afraid to say they had more pleasant things to say of him than most.

Hilbert Gadley worked at Sonn Company most of his life as their accountant, helping with any economic problem that came up, which is always a fun job to have. Money, they say, is the root of all evil, so it is only natural for it to medicate long-term happiness for oneself. I think it is safe to say that all Hilbert knew was the Sonn Company. He never had any other job but that one, being hired right after college and staying on until his final days.

He had a reputation as a loner and kept to himself more often than not, as most loners do. For good reason, since he never had much good to say about anything. Not even a whip about the sports team's losing streak and how they should make a trade or on the local scandal by the town supervisor that is covered in every newspaper, site, and medium the small area can handle. He wouldn't start a conversation that is only spoken of by people to be kind to a stranger rather than any true interest in the words or topic, like the weather. There could be no clouds in the sky, and the sun could be shining, and the day could be that of one where echoes of Shakespeare's sonnet about the summer's day ring over poets' ears, and the block could be blasting the new summer jam that all listeners agree has the feel of summer and welcomes it like they do a cold beverage. The day could be perfect out and on this day, Hilbert would not compliment nature for the greatness and marvel at the beauty of the blueness of the sky and the coolness of the water. Rather, for him, the day would be too hot. When it snowed, I imagined he said it was too cold. I cannot even contemplate that Hilbert had a perfect weather day. All days were bad days for Hilbert, which is as sad of a statement that I could make of a person.

At work, Hilbert didn't pop in on the Friday morning conversation in the break room about the late news and gossip that were being talked about at the office; how the new boss is very strange with his speaking patterns, (what is that accent he is speaking?), or how the saleswoman went to a competitor (do you think she met them at one of the conventions?) When the bi-weekly checks were to be delivered to the employees of Sonn, Hilbert didn't even hand the checks to his co-workers himself. He let his assistant William do so, who found it a great opportunity to flirt with the office secretary rather than a chance to help fellow co-workers.

Hilbert had a family, which is the only reason he kept his job for the first few years. From what I heard, he would have quit a long time ago if it wasn't for his marriage and the birth of his son. Kids do not pay for themselves, and families are not cheap.

Little did Hilbert know that he would lose all his money in the divorce and his son would want no part of him. By the time the boy was eighteen, he packed his things up and moved to Europe. Word on the street is that he married a British woman journalist.

After the heartbreak, which happened long before I was even around, Hilbert married the job he hated and was more alone than ever. By then, his assistant William had long moved on to another job, and Hilbert was left with no assistant and set the checks in a bin for his co-workers to take in their own time. If you hadn't spoken to Hilbert when William was there assisting him in the first few years, then once the guy had worked by himself, there was no way you would even know he had worked at the company. His silence became so apparent that the most he would speak to others was when his co-workers warned new hires not to bother with the old man.

At the time of his death, a time Hilbert was ready for long ago, his ex-wife and former son mourned for him, or so it is said. The fake tears were their best attempt to meet society's standard on how to react to a death in the family.

They really didn't love or care for his passing. Hilbert's wife hadn't seen him since their divorce and brought her banker husband and their four kids to the funeral to show the deceased a family he would never have. The Gadley boy hadn't set foot on American soil since his departure overseas and acted more like a stranger of Hilbert's than his own son. No one knew who he was until he introduced himself. Even then, some guests were unsure of his identity.

Whispers of Hilbert's life were as loud as ever at his funeral. "He had no soul." Lousy old man." "It's about time." He only cared about his job." A few comparisons were made to Ebenezer Scrooge, Scrooge before he met the three ghosts, that is. The whole room was more of a roast for the dead man than any funeral should be. Even the priest was crude as he prepared for a prayer for the deceased. "Let's get this over with. I'll make this short." He said before commanding the room to be silent. The priest said as few words as possible, allowing the Lord's prayer to do most of the talking, as that was as nice a thing anyone could say about Hilbert, which is to not mention him at all.

Unlike most there, I never thought of any of that while sitting in the room with the casket. No. A conversation I had with Uncle Hilbert two weeks prior came to mind. He was ill at the time from all the years of smoking, ill, and still lonely.

Only me and him were in the room as he lay on his deathbed, waiting for the inevitable. My mom, whom I went to go visit him with, was in the kitchen checking on the dinner.

He looked at me with his beaten eyes of a long life of emptiness. It was the first and only time we were alone together. Up until then, I wasn't even aware that he knew of my existence. He spoke with all the power his broken heart and shattered mind could muster. "Do me a favor. Don't be like me." He paused to regain his breath, which gave me a second to be grateful I didn't. "I was wrong. My approach to life. I should have been there for Margaret (his ex-wife), and she found a man who appreciates her, and she's been happy ever since. Joseph (his former son) left for Europe because I neglected him over and over again as a father. I kept trying to buy his love with the little money I had." He turned his head towards the kitchen. "Your mom, she's the only one who comes to see me now. You two are the only visitors I have." He turned back towards me and noticed the shock on my young face. It's not everyday that someone confesses their life's mistakes to you. "I'm telling you this because you still have time." He stared at the wall on the other side of the room and seemed to speak to himself. "God, how youth is wasted on the young." His wrinkly face turned to face mine. "My family gave up on me a long time ago. And for good reason. Sure, they'll show up at my funeral, but they don't have to shed a tear for a selfish old man like me." No longer looking directly, he said, "Promise me this. Don't be like me. Put family first." He paused to regain his breath. "Understand the most important you can give someone is time. Do that before you run out of it. Once today is over, it is gone, and you don't get it back. You can always buy something else or make more money, but the time you have is the most precious thing you can have. Don't waste it like I did."

"Okay," I answered, unsure if I was to say anything else.

"Do what you love. And don't let anyone tell you that you can't do it. Do everything you can for that one dream you have." He paused, having difficulty with his breathing. "I wanted to be a painter as a kid, but my parents and friends said that it was too hard, too much. So I gave it up. There isn't a single day where I don't think about what I could have done if I was a painter."

He seemed to have more to say but stopped, for he was out of breath and out of time.

Shortly after, my mom entered the room with dinner food. The three of us ate together that evening and I listened as Mom and Uncle Hilbert reminisced about times they almost forgot and I've heard before. She did most of the talking and allowed her brother to comment on the story but not strain his voice.

Mom was always able to see the good in people that strangers would pass by. She knew he was mean. She knew he was rotten. She knew he was alone. But she also knew she was family and you must always be there for family, even when that family member did nothing but brought you shame. Not once did I bring up the monologue of Uncle Hilbert. After eating, me and Mom said our goodbyes. It was the last time I ever saw him alive.

When we got in the car, I asked my mom about the situation. "Is he going to die?"

"Yes." She tilted her head back to pull out of the driveway. "He is very sick."

"Oh."

Some time passed before I asked the real question on my mind. "Do people hate Uncle Hilbert?"

She answered in a way. "Your Uncle Hilbert lived a life that was not always favorable in the eyes other family members."

"Then why did we go to see him?"

"Because everyone deserves to see someone who cares for them before they die. I didn't always agree with your uncle, but I knew him when he was younger, and I still believe there is goodness in him. It is in all of us. Some forget they have it. Then the world tells them they don't have it, and after a while, they believe they were never good."

"Oh."

"There is always goodness in someone, no matter how much they think it is gone."

Until now, I never told anybody about the exchange I had with my uncle. About his regret, the sorrow his family shouldn't feel, and how he still felt empty inside after all these years.

The dying wish of my selfish, uncaring, mean uncle was not to be like him. To choose a different path, a more honorable one, from the one he took. That in itself gives me a reason to do so. Self-realization of one's own faults is a noble trait to have. The world remembers my uncle with only harsh episodes and mean digressions, but I will always remember him for the great advice he gave me that I still keep with me to this day.

The Tale of Mr. Will

The Tale of Mr. Will

Before we get to the story, let me ask you a few questions, a few things to jog your mind and perhaps get it running. How would death feel like? Would it hurt to die? Or would it feel like nothing has happened at all? Just a transfer of your soul? Would you know that you died? Or would you have to be told of your death?

See, death is bound to happen to every single one of us, to you, to me, to everyone who has ever heard this tale, has the common thread that they, too, will meet their maker one day. We all know that this is coming, like a storm on the horizon, and we do not know what this feels like. I guess you can only learn of death once you live it.

Let me present you with the tale of Mr. Will. He is the main protagonist of this story and who this is all about. Mr. Will is about as common of a man you can find in that if you were to see him, you would forget that you ever met. Bland face, bland look, all for a bland man.

Whether his name is the first or last is a question, I don't have the answer to at the moment. Is he Mr. Blank Will? Or Mr. Will Blank? For the convenience of the story and to maintain consistency I will direct this man as Mr. Will Blank. Personally, I cannot stand it when a character changes names throughout a story for no reason at all, and I don't have the time or patience to describe my frustration with the matter further. But I digress...

Feeling like he just woke up from a hit on the top of the head, Will did his best to balance his average-sized body in the dark street he found himself in.

He placed both of his hands on the ground and tried to regroup himself from the pain in his head and to put his body in a more comfortable position than it was in. Once his back was straight and his feet no longer needed support from his arms to stay up, he rubbed his eyes with both his hands and spoke to himself, "Jesus Christ." This statement was a reaction to his surroundings more to the man himself.

Before getting to his feet Will examined his surroundings and found he was as close to a black hole as he could be. Nothing there for anybody. Buildings with nothing inside. Sidewalks with no pedestrians. Nothing but the dark of the night.

Oh, and a man in a brown raincoat and hat was leaning against a lamppost while reading the newspaper. The lamp post provided the only light for the whole dark block.
Will got to his feet and tried to figure out what was going on. "Where the hell am I?"

He hoped to find a sign that would easily identify the location he was presently in. Like a person would see when entering a town. Maybe a sign with the slogan "Welcome to Wearevathahelluar." Although the sign would be ironic and not at all comfortable in this otherwise bleak moment, it would provide a starting point for the poor guy. But all Will found was more nothing.
Silence echoed in the night louder than any words could. No wind blew up dust from the ground. No stars shined in the sky. Even the noise made when the man in the raincoat turned the newspaper was so minimal that it was as if he stayed on the same page the entire duration Will gathered his coordinates.

Will commented on the desolate street. "Damn. It's quiet." He walked off the road onto the sidewalk. There, the lamp post shined over the only other individual within walking distance of Will. "This place would use some music. Like Led Zeppelin. Or something."

For the first time Will saw the man in the raincoat leaning up against the lamppost reading the newspaper. He tried to get his attention, "Hey do you know where we are?"
The man in the raincoat glanced for a second at Will and continued reading his newspaper.

Out of the darkness, which seemed to be everywhere and nowhere at the same time, came a terrifying, gruesome scene, which now makes me tremble even as I write it. Floating dark gloves similar to what someone would put on their hands appeared above Will and, with no hesitation, stabbed him in his chest until darkness filled his body. Will fell to the floor and lay in a pool of his own blood. All the while, the man in the raincoat leaned against the lamppost and continued to read the newspaper.

Hey, I told you it was gruesome.

Now, most of you will think that is the end of the tale of Will. He is dead, and nothing more to be said of him. You can all go home and continue on with your days. Perhaps there is a place you need to visit, or perhaps there are some groceries for you to get, but before you leave this tale, I will say that the death of Will doesn't end with him lying in his own blood, not yet.

Feeling like he just woke up from a hit on the top of the head, Will did his best to balance his average-sized body in the dark street he found himself in.

He placed both of his hands on the ground and tried to regroup himself from the pain in his head and to put his body in a more comfortable position than it was in. Once his back was straight and his feet no longer needed support from his arms to stay up, he rubbed his eyes with both his hands and spoke to himself, "Jesus Christ." This statement was a reaction to his surroundings more to the man himself.

Will commented on the desolate street. "Damn. It's quiet." He walked off the road onto the sidewalk. There, the lamp post shined over the only other individual within walking distance of Will. "This place would use some music. Like Led Zeppelin. Or something."

Just then, Will realized his reactions and where he really was. This is the same place where he just died, where he just got stabbed to death, is it not? But if that is the case, then why is he alive, or at least moving without any wounds from the injuries?

"Didn't we do this already?" Will called over to the man in the raincoat, who glanced at Will briefly and continued with his newspaper.

Before he could get his bearings, the same dark gloves hovered over Will and ended his life, filling him with darkness, resulting in his body lying in his own blood. It is still gruesome, and once again the man in the raincoat leaning against the lamppost continued on with reading his newspaper.

This is the part of the story where the readers want to know what is actually happening with what is being told, and this is where I need to remind you that I am nothing more than the narrator to tell you what is going on in the story. I am not here to discuss the whys of what is happening, only to tell you that this is the tale, and this is what happened.

He placed both of his hands on the ground and tried to regroup himself from the pain in his head and to put his body in a more comfortable position than it was in. Once his back was straight and his feet no longer needed support from his arms to stay up, he rubbed his eyes with both his hands and spoke to himself, "Jesus Christ." This statement was a reaction to his surroundings more to the man himself.

Will commented on the desolate street. "Damn... wait I am back here again... and that means that..." He tried to understand the situation he was in.

There is the guy by the lamppost, the empty street, which means only one thing is left to happen to Will.
He looked over at the man in the raincoat who was still reading the newspaper, "Do you plan on helping me this time?"

The man in the raincoat didn't respond, and before Will knew it, he was surrounded by dark gloves that killed him. You know the deal at this point: stabbing, darkness, and Will lying in his own blood.

A bus then drove a few feet from where the man in the raincoat was standing. He closed his newspaper and entered the bus, which had a destination for one place: *Wearevathahelluar.*

And so that is where the story of Will ends, not with him defending himself or learning from his ways, but in the pool of his own blood, as a man who he never met or knew watched him die three times. This tale, like death instead, leaves more questions than answers. Why did Mr. Will die? Where is he? What is going on with the man in the raincoat? And why are those dark gloves stabbing Mr. Will every time they see him?

I can't say I know any of that. I can only say that this is the tale of Mr. Will.

Dream

Dream

How do you describe a dream? Is there a right way to even do it?

We hall had a moment in our life where we are presented with the waking up of a dream, and whether it is real or not, we are stuck with the next question, which is how we even talk about the damn thing. Was that just like a movie? Is that how it was? What about the part where the scenes, if you want to call them that, had no smooth transition? What do you do with the stuff that you kind of recognize but not enough to be sure about it? That one person was someone you knew as a kid, right? Or was it? And if this is a movie, then why is there so much nonsense? I have seen art films, and none of them are as out there as my dreams, so either my dreams are the greatest art films I have ever seen, or dreams are not meant to be seen as movies.

Wait, so it looks like a movie, but it is not a movie because of reasons that the film industry is not even sure about. I say they are dreams, as though that is a proper definition. I am no better than the dictionary, where I define a word with another word.

- Ferocious – to have ferocity

- Ferocity – to be ferocious

But hey, at least we can all agree that the word is either Greek or Latin in origin. Going by how many words are from those two languages, I am think it is safe to say that I speak a broken Greek, or Latin, as much as English. Let's get back to the dream though.

I am then left to talk about a thing that I am not even sure about the definition for, only that the thing that it looks like in my life, is definitely not it. Boy, I am glad that I sleep so many hours every day and I am not even confident with its purpose in my life.

That doesn't even get to the dreams that are just plain out there. You know what I am talking about here. They are the dreams where you are having sex with someone, or you are killed. Should you tell your co-worker that you had a sexual dream about her and that she was pretty wild in it, too? That is bad, right? I mean, if it is only a dream, what is the difference? But then again, the girl may view it very differently. What if you tell that same girl that she killed you in your dreams? What the hell is that about? You wouldn't want to give the girl any ideas.

How do you even start that conversation? As you are putting something in the microwave for lunch, you tell her.

"How was your day? Anything new and exciting happening in your life?" She is waiting for the printer to start working again, as it is down for the second time in as many weeks, so she thought she would pop in and see what is going in the break room.

"I had sex with you in my dreams last night..." You say nonchalantly until you realize that you saw her naked and possibly do things that she would like to keep private, "I mean, you killed me in my dreams. Murdered me like a serial killer. Hack, hack, hack away. That was you. In my dream last night."

"Oh, I was thinking you would tell me more about something related to the job."

"Right..."

What is worse, telling someone that you had sex with them in a dream or that they murdered you in the dream? Both are pretty bad and probably another reason not to share your thoughts on dreams.

Then there are the things or people in the dreams that should not belong. Like the character from the TV show, you have not watched it since you were a kid or the popular figure you have never talked about, ever. They show up in your dream.

Dreams are either too weird for anyone who is listening to them to know what the hell you are talking about, or they are too embarrassing that you want to act as though they never existed.

Who came up with symbols in dreams? That seems like a silly idea, if you ask me, because aren't dreams subjective? Do trains really mean the same thing to everybody? You know what is funny; if you ask people about trains in real life, none of them will give the same answer, but in a dream, we are all expected to think that certain things mean certain symbols.

I don't understand symbols when I am awake; I doubt I will understand them when I am asleep.

Forgetting that dreams have their own separate definition that is not clearly defined, that there are some weird ones that have sex and murder in them, or that there are symbols to these dreams, I wanted to share a dream that I had recently.

I woke up in a sweat one morning to write up this story, not to really describe anything, but to relay what my thoughts had thought that previous night.

Pardon me for anything that is off about this; after all, this is all a dream.

And don't worry, there is no sex or murder in this dream.

I sat in a lavish garden that Louis XIV could have commissioned. The people around me are 18th century aristocrats.

All you need is Mozart's Requiem playing in the background to set the mood for the snobby high class environment. Instead all I hear is a summer hit from the 1990's of a band I could not identify.

I was never one to admire nature, and this time was no different.

Before I could get up from the steps and admire the statues, a black woman who dressed as if she was a different social class than the others walked up to me.

As if she knew me, she stated, "Remember that day?"

I didn't know what she was talking about.

Her eyes focused towards a banner that seemed more fit for a block party that the tea party scene I was in.

I never got a good look at the sign. She continued, "You used the ladder to get out. The water was so bad. It was filled with glass."

I had a vision of walking across a ladder that lay on the water of an upside boat.

Before I could leave, she noticed that my attention was on a woman with a yellow umbrella whom I had never met.

"You never knew, did you? She was in love with another man."

The next sequence of events happened so fast by the time this sentence is done being read they'd have happened.

Everything Must Go

A man in an outfit that Red Coats wore during the Revolution came out of nowhere and shot the maid at point-blank range. A tear ran down my eyes for the friend I lost. And then the Red Coat shot me in the eye.

It felt strange.

Then I was in my bedroom.

My cell phone rang. I let the voicemail get it and walked over to see who called.

It was the president.

I accidentally pressed the play button, and in the message, he spoke of how an alien race of mutated beetles kidnapped him, and this would be his last message because he was going to be killed.

Immediately, I ran to see my parents, who were relaxing on the couch, to see what was going on.

Nervously, I pointed out the weird message I received.

They got it, too.

Turns out the president did a mass relay sort of thing.

Confused, I asked if they believed it.

Without a change of tone in her voice my mom said, "No. It's just a hacker."

Before I could form an opinion on what seemed to be a national crisis, I was underneath a large Oaktree in the middle of nowhere.

A man much older than me, who resembled no one I ever met in my life, stood and admired the leaves on the tree.

"Hello," I said.

"Hi." He answered.

"Where am I?" I asked.

"You don't know?"

"No."

"You are in a dream." He picked up a pot and pan that was on the ground. "Unfortunately for you, I'm the only part of your dream that knows it is a dream." He finished getting his stuff together and balanced the bag on his shoulder. "Yup. It probably could have saved you all the crying and anxiety. But what are you gonna do?"

I reasoned, "But when I got shot. It felt so real. When the phone went off, I really heard it."

"Hey, dreams are powerful stuff, my friend."

"This is a dream, too? So none of this is real?"

"Nope. Sorry to disappoint you."

"Wait. How can you tell me what is real if you aren't?"

He started to walk away. "Let the scientists figure that one out."

"Where are you going?" I asked.

"Oh, I'm going away for a while. But you will see me again. Until then." Walking into the sunset, he yelled back at me. "Dreams are just that ... dreams. It's just you thinking in another way than you're used to. And don't worry about it. You'll wake up eventually."

"But when?" I asked.

He ended it. "Now."

That was it. That was my dream. Was it just like a movie? I guess so...? Will I ever tell this to my female co-worker? No, she quit three months ago and works at a car dealership now. Are there symbols in this dream? If there are symbols in this dream, then there are symbols in just about every dream I ever had.

I am no more certain about what any of it means than you are.

I get up from my desk, being done with my relaying of the dream, "This isn't a dream, right?" I waited for an answer from something. Maybe the president would give me a text message, or that black woman would tell me something I didn't know, but I got nothing.

"This is real because nobody is answering.... At least, I think that is how this goes..."

That is how this goes, right? Don't answer that.

After Meal Message

After Meal Message

"Do you think that French Vanilla comes from France?"

"I don't know," Bret answered, disinterested in the irrelevant question.

Jack took a small sip of his coffee. "I bet Napoleon had a hand in it. He seems to be a part of France's history in every way. I know he helped America with the Louisiana Purchase. It turns out war doesn't pay for itself."

Bret's mind was somewhere else at the moment as he was not paying any attention to the possibility of the famous

French king being involved with a coffee creamer. "Yeah, sure."

"The guy had his own code and crowned himself king; I'm pretty sure he had a say in coffee creamer."

"Whatever." Bret failed to make eye contact with his company at the restaurant booth.

Jack finally picked up on his friend's indifference to their conversation. "What's the matter? You didn't order anything, and now you haven't even had any of your coffee. You okay?"

When the two men arrived a little earlier Bret declined to order any sort of food from the menu. As compared to Jack whose order of a bacon, egg, and cheese burrito with fries and coffee was enough for any person. Bret would not have gotten anything, but received a cup of coffee because the waitress mistakenly gave him one as well.

"I haven't been feeling too good since that car accident."

This was the first time Jack had heard of this. "When did you get into a car accident?"

"Earlier today, around nine."

"It couldn't have been that bad since you made it here. Where was it?"

There were no noticeable marks on Bret's body from the crash. No cuts from shattered glass, no bruises from a cement fall, not an injury he suffered from his unfortunate collision.

"It was in the middle of the street on Port Jefferson Road, by the new bank they put in."

"What new bank? There is a new one built every other week. Did you see the ones off the parkway that are across the street from each other? I'm telling you, I should have been a banker." He took a sip of his coffee. "But then again, I have a soul."

"You know the bank. I can't think of its name." Bret snapped his fingers. "It is the one with green and black colors."

Jack tried to imagine in his head the location of the accident. "I don't know where you are on Port Jefferson Road. Are you past the Chinese restaurant we go to sometimes?"

"Yeah. It is further down the road than that."

"Past the community park?"

"Yeah. Right by there. By the playground side of the park, not by the basketball and tennis courts."

"Oh. I think I know where you are. So how did it happen?"

"They started from the bottom, I assume. How else do you start something like that?"

"No. I mean the car accident. How did that happen?"

"Oh. Well, I was on one of those yellow lanes crossing the street."

"So you were walking in the middle of the road? You know when you do that, your chance of getting hit goes up exponentially? That is why there are those walkways. Who knew they weren't just for show? Pretty soon, you'll tell me that the red lights have a purpose too."

"Those yellow lanes are fine to stay on for a little bit to cross the street. They are like sidewalks. People walk on them all the time."

"Says the guy who got hit while standing on them."

"I was standing there waiting for an opening to cross the street, and a... bus came."

"To get in the lane that you shouldn't have been in, to begin with. I can't stand when those buses do what they are supposed to do."

"Yeah. When that includes almost ending my life, so do I."

"And then it hit you, I presume. There is a part of this story where you hit a car, right? You didn't end up running up to a car in the parking lot just to make up for surviving, did you?"

"No. When I ran away from the bus, I ran into the intersection, and that is when I got hit by a Sedan."

"Wait. I thought you said you ran away from the bus. I know speed isn't your thing, but ..."

"I did try to avoid the bus. But I ran this way, not that way." Bret motioned his hand in a poor explanation of the crash. What he was trying to say is that he ran in the same direction that the bus was going rather than cutting across to another lane with no cars.

"That's dumb. You should have gone in another lane to miss the bus altogether."

"Now I know that. It wasn't really on my mind when a bus was coming at me full speed. What do I look like to you, one of those expert stunt people? You caught me. I actually take stunt classes each weekend. This week, we will go over a new maneuver technique to get in a van that goes at sixty miles per hour."

"Well, at least you're okay." Jack realized who he was talking about. "Relatively speaking."

"Yeah. One's well-being is normally subjective."

Jack shook his head in disagreement with his friend's choice. "I can't believe you trust people enough to stand in the middle of the road as they drive by. Have you not met people? These are the same people who take showers in water and then run away when droplets come down from the sky. These people get lost using a GPS, and they think that a flea market has actual fleas. These are the people you trust your life with while standing in the middle of a busy road? Let me ask you this: would you trust yourself, if you were driving, to not hit a person standing in the middle of the road?"

"I think I am pretty trustworthy. One time, a co-worker asked me to keep her pregnancy a secret, and I did, for a whole day."

"Who?" Jack took another sip of his nearly finished cup of coffee. "Oh wait, I remember you told me once. It was that cute girl in the office. Wait, but didn't she tell you because it was yours?"

"At this point, I am more worried about recovering from this accident. Then I can get back to." He paused. "that."

Lauren walked into the restaurant and spotted her friends at the second booth. Before she could even sit down, Jack asked her about his creamer, pondering. "Do you think French Vanilla comes from France?"

She sat in the booth seat across from Bret and put her pocketbook on her side. "I don't know. Who cares?"

"I thought that since Napoleon had such an influence on France's history, he might have had a say."

"This is what you think about in your spare time." She reached over the table to look at the menu. "I am sure someone cares about the answer to your question, but I'm not that person. If the answer doesn't affect me, then I find it irrelevant to know."

Bret changed the topic. "Did something happen? What took you so long to get inside? We have been here for fifteen minutes already."

"I already ordered."

"Thanks for waiting." She continued to go over the menu.

"You're welcome."

She flipped the menu over and realized it was the wine and dessert list.

"This is the wrong menu." She put it back. "Anyway, there are no parking spots. I had to park across the street. I was going to park in the handicap spot, but I thought it was unnecessary."

"You didn't want to feel guilty about blocking the accessibility for those who are incapable of moving too far?"

"No. I hate to back up when leaving, and the only way to get into the spot was to go straight into it. Besides parallel parking, backing up is the worst part of driving. There is always one idiot who cuts me off."

"Bret should tell you about his accident."

Before the car accident victim could speak, Lauren gave her thoughts on his accident. "Please tell me the poor woman knows. Cause that is the sleaziest thing a man can do. You have sex with a woman because that thing of yours goes crazy, and then you leave as soon as the kid arrives. As soon as you have to stop thinking of yourself and that thing of yours, you bail. What is her name? Is she the one we met at your office party? She is kind of cute, I guess. Still, you know I didn't think you were one of those..."

"It is not that kind of accident." Bret stopped Lauren before she could go further.

"What happened? Did you stub your toe or slip while going up the stairs? If you did, then let's talk about that vanilla creamer."

"The man crowned himself king!" Jack exclaimed.

"I got into a car accident on Port Jefferson Road before getting over here."

"Port Jefferson Road? Where is that?"

"Really?" Jack was taken aback by Lauren's ignorance of the familiar road.

"We drive on it whenever we get Chinese food."

"Oh. That road. I don't go by road names. I only know landmarks."

"That's a relief since those don't change at all." A waitress brought over Jack's order of a bacon, egg, and cheese burrito with fries. "Oh boy. Look at this."

"Hi. Can I have some French toast and sausage and a coffee?" The waitress took Lauren's order and headed back to the kitchen. "You know Bret you are lucky to be alive."

"Am I?"

"Eh." Both Lauren and Jack shrugged their shoulders.

"Anyone who says they are lucky to be alive is not living. They have reached the point in their life where all they can do is reminisce about their past to make their boring present more bearable. I'm convinced that when I die, when my time comes to leave this god-awful place, Death will look at me and my miserable existence and say, "Come on you.""

Jack quickly responded. "As compared to saying what? Talking in sign language? Do you think that Death will sing you a song when you leave?"

"When I die, the first thing I am going to do is ask Death about that awful outfit. I mean, a black cloak? It's so dated. And that scythe is so useless. Why carry that thing around everywhere he goes? What purpose does it even have?"

Jack was stuffing his face with his meal. "What's wrong with a black cloak?"

"It's obvious that Death is ugly and unattractive and feels insecure about it, so it hides its face whenever it can. If Death was attractive, do you think it would hide it? No. It would flaunt its beauty."

"I always thought Death was a skeleton." Bret brought up nonchalantly.

"What?" Lauren gave Jack a napkin to keep tidy. "Thanks."

"Yeah. Isn't that why he wears a cloak, to cover up his bones? Underneath that cloak is nothing but a skeleton, not a human with any organs or skin."

"Now, see, that is a very typical man thing to do. You assume that the character is a man when you have no proof that it is. Why can't Death be a woman? We are every bit capable of being the Messenger of Souls as you are."

"Oh, come on." Jack stopped eating for a second. "Like a woman would want to go around to all the deceased and tread them off to hell. Think about all the different types of corpses you would have to deal with. It is disgusting. Face it. It is a man's job; dull, lethargic. Plus, you said it: if Death was a woman, his fashion sense would be better."

"I am going to the bathroom before my food comes out." Lauren got up and headed to the women's restroom at the other end of the restaurant.

A tall, black, cloaked figure walked into the restaurant and sat at the open booth seat previously held by their woman friend. The figure tapped his skeleton fingers on the table a few times before directing his attention to Bret. "You ready?"

Bret looked at the only other human with skin at the table, one whose mouth was filled with cheese. "Look. I have to go."

Jack put down his food for a moment to say a coherent goodbye. "Okay. I'll see you tomorrow and let Lauren know you left."

"Yeah. Thanks."

Bret put his jacket on and got up alongside the figure. Before either move towards the door, the cloaked figure pointed out Bret's table manners.

"You gonna throw that out?" Bret begrudgingly picked up his still-full cup of coffee and put it in the bin by the garbage. "Don't be a slob. No one likes a slob."

The two walked towards the exit and headed into the parking lot.

"This is me." The figure pointed to a black limousine in the handicap parking space. "How did your friends take the news?"

"Good. Good."

"It should be unlocked." The figure got into the driver's seat as Bret stood there waiting because of the scythe in the passenger seat. "Oh, let me get that out of your way." The figure tossed his weapon in the back seat. "If you want to scare someone, then bring out this baby, and they won't hesitate to come along with you. Would you believe that this is more effective at terrifying dead souls than a gun? I know, right?" The figure starts the car as Bret puts on his seatbelt. "You really think this cloak is outdated? I find the blackness adds intimidation to my presence. For a few years, I tried silver, but that didn't have the same effect on people."

"It looks fine. Your cloak is very fashionable. I wish I had one myself." Bret stared blankly into the distance through the front mirror.

The figure turned around in his seat and began to back the limo out of the spot. "I got to hurry on out of here. I parked in the handicap spot, plus I have to be back here a little later today."

Pat's Birthday (Two Girlfriends)

Pat's Birthday (Two Girlfriends)

Patrick Tavin has never thrown a baseball around with his father his whole life, not even once. Never did he go to the park on a spring day with a glove in hand, ready for an afternoon of catch. He barely knows what baseball is. The only team he knows of is the New York Yankees, and anyone can recognize the pinstripes.

During recess, Patrick would sit on the side wall as the rest of the athletically astute kids played kickball. He attends the elementary school JFK, which most would assume is named after the assassinated victim who just so happened to be president, but that is not so. It really stands for "Jail for Kids." That is going by the students of the K-5 school, so who knows? Anyway, JFK gym teachers find it easier for the kids to play kickball at recess than baseball. There are much fewer wild pitches when the ball is rolled, although unbelievably, there are still a few. Also, the gym teacher, Mrs. Feltlee, could check to see if anyone was stuck on the monkey bars instead of tossing a softball to a kid who could barely stand up straight, let alone swing a baseball bat. That's without mentioning the lack of knowledge the students had for the game. There always seemed to be a few kids who would run the wrong way around the bases if they hit the ball or they'd somehow throw it backward. Add all that to the incident that happened in New Field a few years back, where a kid sitting on the wall got hit by a baseball bat that went further than the ball, and I'd say the school has a good reason to let the kids play kickball at recess instead of baseball. Even if baseball was a favorable pick among the students of Jail For Kids, a recent law has been passed that prohibits baseball from being played at recess. It can only be played during the class, where there is a supervisor at all times for the students. It was passed because of the outcry by the New Field parents. They claimed the school should have taken more precautionary measures to ensure the safety of the child. I'm not sure how the school would do that, but the law is there nevertheless, so whenever Mrs. Feltlee is teaching baseball she is practicing how not to get hit by a ball and die as much as the game itself. Per usual, our politicians have done their best to help everyone.

Whether the cause of the lack of baseball in Patrick's life is the result of the great encouragement his school gave him, Patrick's quiet, timid nature, or the fact that there is no father figure in his life to push it upon him is unclear. Patrick's mother, Denise Tavin, knows a lot about the game of baseball and is against the act of the New Field. The game of baseball has something other sports cannot teach. It teaches hand-eye coordination and proper arm strength, which is great for a young child to learn. Plus, the incident at New Field could be a result of the game not being taught as much as a cause of it. If the kids knew how to play the game, then they wouldn't have been hurt. It is because the kids are not being taught how to play that the bat is flying from the hand of a kid.

Denise was quite the athlete in her youth. She could recollect memories of her younger years when she would hit for singles and doubles in her high school games and where she traveled to in college because of her softball scholarship. She could bring up her dislikes in the evolution of the game and how the emphasis on bringing in the closer and hitting home runs ruined "real" baseball. She has even made the argument that Pete Rose, the notorious enemy in baseball for gambling on the sport, should be allowed in the Hall of Fame, and if Cooperstown lets the Steroid guys in, then the game is hurt for it. She believes that baseball can't ignore the Steroid Era and the farce it was, and has on numerous occasions thought they should make a separate wing for the corrupt age, teaching the fans of the game's mistakes when it all was wrong. The players took drugs to get ahead. The league and others in the know turned their heads because the game was booming. All was wrong in the game: the players for cheating and the league and other outlets for ignoring it. And why? Because of the root of all evil, and the very same reason that you see organizations and institutions get brought into court: money. For what are morals and integrity if you can buy all that you need with money? You can motivate a man to do great things with wise words, but you can control him with money, which is exactly what the Steroid Era did.

They thought they had it all planned out, too, like a train robber with their setup route, the train they would rob, and the proper crew who had all the skills needed. They even had a passenger on the train in on the entire robbery in case things went wrong. It was all planned out, and it should have been easy. We should not know what the Steroid Era in baseball even is, and yet we are talking about it because somewhere, somehow, a force that is beyond even that of a baseball player made their actions wrong. You can trick the world into thinking that you are right with your wrong deeds, but you can never fool the truth that you spread lies. The truth always wins, even though it appears it is never really fighting sometimes.

Denise could talk about all of that, but she knows her son has no interest. Teaching Patrick to throw a baseball or to pick up a ground ball (she had quick hands, for she was a second baseman in her day) was something best to leave for the boy to see and observe if that much. Her motherly instincts told her that Patrick was more the studious type anyway. That could be an acknowledgment of Patrick's poor coordination as much as it is a recognition of his average mind.

Sitting down on the living room couch with his crossed legs on the table, Patrick closed the book his mother bought him for his birthday with the money she had left over from working three jobs. A Dr. Seuss book is the best Denise could afford right now for her little boy. Patrick has read *Green Eggs and Ham* four times while waiting for his mom to get ready. He was hesitant to start the book a fifth time since the plot didn't change the first four times he read it. They normally don't.

The two were to go out to Patrick's favorite food place Nathan's to celebrate his birthday. Ever since the one in the Home Depot down the road closed a few years back they only go once a year since the closest one is now an hour away. That is if Denise drives 80 miles an hour. It is only a matter of time before that Nathan's goes out of business too.

After putting the book on the side of his left hip, Patrick picked up the remote controller and pressed the buttons at a pace so fast that if you asked what he watched, he would be able to name only a few of the thirty or forty he went through. Denise walked by the living room and noticed her son's attention was no longer on his gift and was treating the living like his bedroom. "Get your feet off the table." Obeying his mother's demand, Patrick reluctantly slid his feet off the table. "What happened? No more green eggs?"

"They make me hungry." Patrick doesn't understand that no one in their right mind would eat green eggs and ham and that Sam-I-Am is either the worst chef in the world who doesn't know the basics for a good meal and is putting his friend in danger by feeding him such food or he is some diabolical cook bent on using rhymes and annoying his friend until the poor guy decides to eat the food that will most likely kill him. There was no sequel to Green Eggs and Ham since the eater in the book probably died from food poisoning and Sam-I-Am went to prison. I want to say that the meal has a symbolism to it that an adult could grasp later in life, but I don't know if that is the case. The whole book and story are nonsensical rhymes that kids love. In other words, the book makes complete sense to kids.

Denise exited the living room, and Patrick went back to clicking. He continued the rigorous exercise of his thumb and the brainwashing of his youthful mind until the remote slipped out of his tiny fingers and under the table he once had his feet on. Stuck with the decision to crawl under the dusty table or pick up *Green Eggs and Ham* a fifth time, he crawled. He could have left the remote under the table and sat there content, watching the *People's Court*, where a contractor is being sued by a client for not completing the job properly, but he didn't even contemplate that option. Getting on his hands and knees in a quick motion his feeble body would allow, Patrick examined the floor under the table. It was then, for the first time, that he saw a large red dot from the fruit punch he spilled a month ago that he had never cleaned up. Along with the red dot were other decaying matter on the rug that time got the best of. He spotted the remote, which wasn't very hard since it was the only clean object down there in the last fifteen years. Next to the remote was a bunch of books that were too advanced for someone Patrick's age, even the studious type. They blended in with the dusty tan floor, and one book caught Patrick's eye. It had no paper cover, usually found on books, and had a dark blue cover, and the only words on it were in gold print, all capitalized *Two Girlfriends*. There was no author to speak of. Most readers of an older age may notice the peculiarity of a book having no author, but Patrick did not. He thought that was how the book was supposed to look.

Patrick reached for the remote and the book he never heard of. To Patrick, any book was better than *Green Eggs and Ham* again. The eater never declines the green eggs and ham. No matter how much you read that book and think that he may stick to his guns, he doesn't. He eats the ham.

The birthday boy got up from under the table, and to say he was a little dusty would be an understatement. You would have thought the kid had gone out of his way to get dust on his clothing instead of only going underneath the table. Denise poked her head in to check on her son and make sure he wouldn't end up like that kid from New Field. She noticed his messy clothes from his crawl with the dust bunny.

"You're a mess." She did her best to make her son's appearance presentable. Denise was not satisfied with his dusty clothes but was in no mood to grant him liberty to run to his room and choose his own outfit. She knew he would pick the worst combination of clothing possible. She didn't want him dressed that way for his birthday, so she gave him his jacket and advised him, "Wear this. It's cold out today."

Denise knew that the worst thing a kid could do, aside from getting hit with a baseball bat during recess, was to not have on a coat in order to prevent the cold. This was the one motherly issue she had with the kid, as much as anything else. She was fine with her little boy not liking the sport she loved or that he was of an average mind that would be lucky to get a job one day. If there is one thing that Patrick will do, it is wear a coat when it is cold outside. That is the one thing that Denise is good at telling the boy.

She started to walk to the hallway to finish getting ready for lunch, but before she could leave her son's vision, he asked about the book under the table. "Mommy. What's this?"

She was still getting ready, putting on her earrings and a rather sharp dress for a fast food place like Nathan's. Only she knew she had a date at the home later that night. She did not feel compelled to tell Patrick about her dating his teacher, Mrs. Feltlee. Denise turned to see what he was talking about. "Oh, nothing. Let me have it." She was grateful for his quietness being that of a mime.

"Is it you?" By that, Patrick meant whether his mother was one of the girlfriends. He did not ask because he had evidence of his mother but because he was just curious.

Covering up her tracks well, she told her son to continue reading his favorite book, to which he replied it only made him hungrier.

Just then, Denise dashed back into the hallway to see a face, a young woman's face. It was not Mrs. Feltlee's but Jacklyn Harris's, the college student who lives down the block. Now you can see why Denise was taking extra long to get ready this time. She snuck Jacklyn, who still had her backpack on, out the back door in no view of her son, trying to be as casual as possible and hoping his naïve mind would miss a few things of her adult life. Relieved and taking a deep breath, Denise watched for a while to give Jacklynn time to get a head start. As a little sweat poured from her face, Denise stayed put in order so they would not meet outside. A situation she wanted to avoid since an explanation would have to be given to her son, an explanation she didn't want to give. Not much time had to pass because Denise wasn't alone in keeping the secret. Jacklyn ran home when leaving the Tavins, even though she convinced her parents Miss Tavin was her tutor, which she was in a way I will not go into. Jacklyn's parents believe the two meet cordially for an hour to discuss problems she is having in her classes. This time was well past the hour limit, and the last thing Jacklyn wanted to do was tell her parents about her tutor lessons.

Denise closed her eyes, almost falling asleep right there, until she heard a familiar voice call out, "Mommy. I'm ready." She was not ready at all but was ready to get out of the stressful situation she was in.

She kneeled down to be at eye level with her son and spoke in an energetic voice to capture the youth's attention. "Who is ready for Nathan's? I think I am going to have the hot dogs. What about you?"

The answer was irrelevant for most people know Nathan's for their hot dogs and most go with the intent on getting the food. Patrick did not catch the deliberation in his mother's statement.

Keeping her son away from the door, she opened the front door to check if her college friend left. Ignoring his mother's questions, Patrick asked, "Why was the girl who lives down the block here?'

Stunned by her son's awareness, Denise tried to get him to talk about the birthday gift he had left on the couch. "Don't forget your green eggs." She lunged across the couch, nearly ripping her dress to reach the conversation changer.

"Mommy, is she your girlfriend?"

Not sure is she would tell the truth about her two girlfriends Denise told him advice on how to handle it. "Make sure your buttoned up. There's a chill outside."

The End of Life

The End of Life

Before I begin this short piece, this tale of a family, this digression of life, I would first like to ask the reader a question, if they don't mind, what is one more question that we all have as we slope the avalanches of our days unsure if we are climbing or merely falling? *What is a miracle?* How do you identify such an event? Can you identify the miraculous with words like the ones you read before you, and if you were a gifted oracle, how would you respond to its appearance in your life? A miracle is not like postage arriving in the mail that you unpack and never think of again. The momentous occasion stays with you long afterward, almost performing a second miracle in staying in your memory for so long. Would you convert your repetitive, bland ways and become a new person? Or ignore the fateful message as mere coincidence and go back on scientific data to prove that a very episode in your life was false. Or perhaps you see miracles in a different light, as not a moment of resurrection or of spiritual awakening but of life itself. The air that you breathe gives you the love you feel that you can then communicate in the words you know. The miracle of life is that there is life at all, and you are here to be a part of that strange, elusive experience. Although this is a very popular belief among non-theists, it fails to recognize the person who does not see life this way, who sees miracles as single events, not as an outlook. What of the man who claimed to see heaven when he was pronounced dead? What of the woman who says she saw the Lord in a vision? What about the soldier who got shot straight in the chest yet lived to talk about it? All logic tells us that the man who saw heaven should have been dead. Once the machine goes off and your heart stops pumping, you should no longer come back into this world and enter the darkness of life because your body is expired. Yet, he did breathe a second time and claimed to see a place that many only know of in words. The woman does not even know who Christ is, so she shouldn't be talking to him. She is no Christian. She has little faith. So why is she convinced that on one lonesome night, the Lord, who I am sure the reader is aware of, came to her and spoke in the same way, I speak to you? The soldier should be buried in the ground as his comrades commemorate the heroism he displayed for his country. The human body cannot stand certain acts, like a bullet to the chest, where the heart lies, yet the soldier took the bullet wound as if the shot was not fatal. Against all the numbers, all the equations, all the reasoning, the miracle prevails, overcoming not only the odds but our very belief in them.

We enter the scene of a husband and wife arguing as they prepare dinner. The wife, Anne, makes chicken and rice meals for the family of three because they all want to eat edible food. She has been the family's cook ever since they formed since her husband Wilson knows nothing about dinner. This is not the first time that Anne has made this meal for the family, so no one, not her, Wilson, or Paul, their child of 8 years, complains. Speaking as an eater, for a second, I can say that although chicken and rice are quite simple meals, I do find them quite satisfying for my taste buds. But I digress; Wilson contributes to the meal in a way that he can with his limited knowledge of preparing food by setting up a small table with utensils and plates.

Recently, the two adults had an event that they deemed to be a miracle. This event was experienced by the two of them, and we come into the conversation as they change topics, playing that one to death since the miracle that was (or wasn't) is all that has been on their mind the past week. *What does it mean? What should they do about it? Was it even* real? As for the details of the miracle, which I am sure you would like to know more about, I will let your imagination decide that.

"So what you are saying is that it doesn't matter if he is spiritual?" The husband asked of the wife's intent.

"No. But he should choose for himself. The soul knows what it wants."

"Choose? Choose? This isn't a game show with a few trivia questions. He can't take a few seconds to pick a category he knows." He imitated a game show contestant. "Hmm... Let me see, Alex; I will take Things I Know for 1000."

"So you want us to push this on him? What message does that send him that he must be dictated to his faith rather than receive it from within and above? Is it true spirituality if the person doesn't get it naturally?"

"What if he chooses wrong?" Wilson asked as he got the plates down on the table first. "What if he sides with The Devil and his trickery? What if he rejects the miracles he sees? What if he doesn't listen to his heart, or worse, it lies to him?"

"He won't. He is our son, so he has our blood in him. He talks like us. He thinks like us. He is one of us. We are full of hope, and so is he." She continued to cook the rice.

"I just worry for him, is all. Mind getting me some cups?" He asked as his wife reached over to the cabinet with cups and handed him three stacked together. "Thanks."

"So do I, but he will be alright. You must have faith that he will be. That is why they call it faith; you must abandon your reasoning and trust that a higher power will lead the way."

"Yeah, it's just, you know, when Adam and Eve were given the option of choice, they made the wrong decision right away."

"Good thing we don't have any snakes then."

The skeptical husband had finished setting up the table as the wife was done with the rice. Next up was grilled chicken.

"I'll go check on the little rugrat." The husband exited the kitchen and walked into the living room to find his son staring at the TV.

"What are you watching?" He asked his youthful kid, Paul.

"I don't know."

"You don't know what is keeping your mind occupied? And that doesn't bother you?"

"It's a show," Paul answered, eyes fixated on the screen.

"Do you not know what you read when you open a book? Are the words foreign to you as your eyes scan the page? Do you not know what you listen to when you hear a song? Are you tuning out the words of the singer for a few minutes as you tune into the radio? How do you not know what can take up so much of your time? Are you not going to know where you are going when you step into the car? How about not knowing your food as you eat it? Don't be so mindless, son. The world is more than happy to waste your mind, so don't go wasting it for them."

Paul looked towards the kitchen. "Mom! Dad's talking weird again!" The kid called out to his mom in the other room, who didn't answer.

"Talking weird? Is that what you kids call it when people form more than a few sentences together? You spend all day watching garbage, developing no original thoughts of your own or meaningful data for your future, and yet I am the weird one. Perhaps I am. Not many think in this world. To have an original idea is quite strange in this world of phonies, copycats, and frauds. The original thinker stands out more than a horse among zebras, seeking comfort in their company but never truly knowing it, for who they are cannot be taken away. If to talk weird is to think, then I..." He noticed his son staring back at the TV, not listening to him. "We'll be eating in a little bit."

The dad left the room, leaving his son to watch what was on the screen.

An old man in shades sat on a lawn chair in the middle of nowhere, finishing up his lunch of a hamburger with a soda. He slowly ate away at the burger and drank his soda. What is time to this man? What is time to any man? Why worry about it all? Time will pass, regardless of what you, or me, or anyone does about it. Once it is his time, he'll know, and then he'll leave this place, no questions asked. What is time? That's just a way for you to know how much you have left.

And this man knows he is almost done.

Yes, through all of his experience, from the beginning, where he worked too hard, from the betrayal, where his good friend hurt him, to his many friends that filled his life with personality and joy, to his son that he loved so much, this guy has been through a lot, and it is safe to say that this will be his last meal.

He took a bite out of his hamburger.

Remember the beginning? Man, that was something else. He worked all week for the start of things, so much so that he decided to take a break on the last day of the week. Now, normally, he doesn't mind working hard and putting in some OT hours to get what needs to get done, but that week was something different. There was nothing there. He had to start from scratch, and boy, did it take more out of him than he ever expected. If you work too hard, you become stale and uninspired, exhausted and apathetic, and you lack the originality and creativity that so many jobs need in order for them to be done effectively. Taking that last day off to relax and get his stuff together was the best thing he ever did. Sometimes, this old man knows how to help himself, and creating something from nothing while still giving himself an off day was one of those moments.

He took another bite out of his burger.

Do you remember the fall? Man, that was some sad stuff right there. His greatest ally, who he loved so much, turned on him and then became his enemy. The crazy guy thought he could do the old man's job. And he was wrong. Now that guy, if he even is one, at this point, is still mad and bummed about how it all went down. He asked for a fight, got one, and lost big time, and he is still mad about losing. Talk about being a sore loser. After the fight where he had to kick out his greatest ally, the ally is still pissed at him, even though the two haven't spoken in years. Damn, after a while, you'd figure that the crazy guy would let the whole thing go. Move on. You lost. You aren't as great as you thought you were. But does he? No. Some people, man, you just can't get through to them. Hardball is the only game they want to play, and then they get mad when you beam them with a fastball for staying too close to the plate.

He took a sip out of his soda.

Remember all his friends? That's quite a list right there. All those who he knew over the years who really made his life the great journey that he looks back on now. I mean, did he need these people? Eh…. Not really, but they do put a smile on his face when he thinks of them. There was that guy on the boat. The guy with the bow and arrow. The really rich guy who thought too much of himself. The really strong guy. There was that guy who left his home with all his people. That isn't even half of it all. He misses those friends. Good times, man, good times. All of his friends had a purpose; they all tried to help him out along the way.

He took another sip out of his soda.

Remember his son? That boy prodigy turned out alright. He is damn proud of what that boy has done for so many people. It makes it all worthwhile knowing that his greatest achievement was the best person many saw. He is still surprised that the boy was so great. I mean, he knew he would be great, but he was even better than he expected. The old man is always happy to think of the guy that he gave this world. No one is quite like him or ever will be. Not to brag, but he is quite the dad. Probably the best.

The old man finished up his meal as he recalled memories of his time, of all time.

For a moment, he relaxed by the nothingness around him. Sometimes, you need to hear the sound of silence to understand the noise. Nothing can say so much to your mind and soul if you are willing to listen. More than the many sounds of life that we all listen to intently. The meal eater could never understand why people didn't like being alone in all the silence. Many who are afraid of truth run from the very notion, as if the silence makes them a weirdo or a strange individual. But it doesn't. They are only worried about the truths that the silence says to them. Silence has no bias. It feels nothing of your good or bad. It is not impressed by your victories or upset over your setbacks. It simply speaks whispers of truth to your ears, informing you of the world as it is, not the world you wish to see. Many people, from the young and naïve to the old and stupid, should try to find that quiet room and enjoy the silence it gives them rather than looking for parties and friends who disturb it.

He leaned back on the lawn chair and then dozed off, dreaming of his life and the many good times that he had.

When he woke up from the nap, he got up from his chair, refreshed from the little shut-eye he got.

The senior stretched out a little bit to loosen up his fragile body. The bones aren't as strong as they used to be. His skin isn't as smooth as when he started everything. But does he allow that to stop him? No. for the physical body is just that, physical and limited to the restraints of time. He knows that his spirituality and mental state will always be with him, for time cannot hold them back.

He stretched his back first, hearing a few cracks. Then he shook his hands and then his feet until he felt like he was ready to get up one last time.

After stretching, he sat back down in his chair, thinking of his next move, of his last move, of the move that he planned on doing when he began everything. Before the beginning, the fall of his ally, the help from his friends, and his one son, which made him proud, he planned his move, the end.

Before there was even a beginning, there was an end.

"It's about time." He said.

On the table next to him was a box marked "SOUNDS." He flipped through the papers in the box and picked up a folder marked "MUSIC."

He opened up the record player on the table and put the record inside. He folded the lawn chair and leaned it up against the tiny table of the record player and the plate that once held his food.

He turned as if talking to the camera that wasn't there. "That's it, folks. The show is over. "

"I'm out." He called out to the nothingness.

The old man walked away from the music recorder. He picked up his now folded lawn chair and headed off into the setting sunset.

He took one last look at the audience that isn't there. "Thanks for watching, everyone."

Then he snapped his fingers, and the song "Ob-La-Di, Ob-La-Da" by the

Beatles played as the credits roll.

Life

Created by God

Produced by God

With Special Help from Jesus and the Holy Spirit.

Also, special thanks to all the angels and saints in heaven.

Then, a list of every person who had ever lived appeared in the order that they first appeared.

The dad walked in as the show was ending. "It's time for dinner. So how was your show? Did you get the name of it? Maybe even some plot?"

The child looked at his father, "No. I didn't get it. He just left the stuff there."

The dad shook his head as his son entered the kitchen. "Kids...

The Merchant of Death 💀

The Merchant of Death

The world has ended, and all of life was destroyed. We have become nothing but ash in a lone field with no wind to blow or pile to become, a vacant body with no home to settle or burial to sleep in, a lost cause of no meaning or purpose for the beliefs we held. The world is nothing with the very life that inhabits it. Sure, there is a world without life. The plants shall always be growing on the ground. The sun shall always be shining. The water will always be splashing on the shores. But with no soul of the human to interact with the world, what does the world even have? Nothing but empty sounds and heartless movements. The human soul, with its witty laughter, wholesome community, and organized chaos, creates a way for the world to cherish. Without it, the world might as well not be. This world has ended. Well, besides me, the narrator of this piece. The bard of the composition. The man you are stuck listening to for the next few minutes. If life had ended, then I wouldn't be able to tell you this story. So, as I said, the world has kind of ended, and life has merely changed. I am covered in ashes from dust to dust. I am here to tell you how it happened.

I'm no scholar or man of sophistication, but I believe the technical term for what happened is called "nuclear war."

A bomb went off. And it was a big one. It destroyed all in that small country, I forget its name, somewhere near an ocean, and that bomb led to famine for the country and the rest of the world. That led to unrest until

two more bombs went off. From what I remember, the major powers of the world were trying to control their tempers between each other and the madness that had occurred within their own borders, and they came to the conclusion that dropping a bomb on their enemy would solve the problem. I believe they thought irrationally that by eliminating their enemy, they could better focus on the problems the world was facing. They were wrong. The two bombs destroyed just about everyone left on this planet. Whatever hope that the world had for getting through the first bomb ended when the second two went off within a few hours of each other. I am not going to give you a rundown of the whole event, but long story short, I am stuck wondering about this wasteland of a world with nothing more than my wits and what is on my back.

I now spend my days searching for life on this planet, for there are not many of us left to live here. Or to die as many would see it. I wander from road to road to town to town looking for whoever I can, for those of the past that called this place home too. So far, the mission has been a failure. I have found nobody in the many places and homes that I scavenged.

Early on, I recognized this problem of aloneness, in that by staying put, I can only meet a survivor who comes to me, so I decided the best course of action was to not create a home set in one place, for I may never find anyone that way. I am a nomad in the sincerest sense of the word. I couldn't risk staying in a random home that I found and trying to find someone. I had to at least try.

One late night, after another day of finding no one, I tried to fix the radio that I had set up. It is not the most advanced piece of equipment that I can use, and I am currently trying to find more advanced materials, but I have not been successful in that endeavor. All that I have found has been broken or not functional, and I have not found any other pieces that could make the new equipment work. So, I am stuck with the modest radio that I broadcast to anyone who can hear.

What started out as a simple fix turned into a more diligent task that; I had to stop what I was doing in order to proceed. I knew how to fix this radio to get it to work. I have done it many times before. Most fixes need a minor adjustment, like a new piece. Nothing that I can't solve. When I have to fix the radio in ways that I cannot fully understand and that take a while, I don't enjoy doing it late at night, when I am already exhausted, so I set aside a day for the project so that it can be the one thing I have my attention. If this were in the morning, I wouldn't be so anxious to end the fix, but it was night, and I was in no mood for it. After yet another failed attempt at fixing the radio, I threw the piece I was trying to install against the wall in frustration. "You piss of shit! Goddamnit! This part is supposed to fit. I know that I fixed this before." I pounded the floor, causing my hand to bleed. I stopped after I felt the pain, and I put a towel over the blood. I took a few deep breaths as I sat down, bleeding from my own blood and patience. "What the hell am I doing? What am I doing here? There is no one out there. There is no one but me left in this world. I am all alone. Why am I even fixing this damn thing? What am I doing here? Does anybody know?" I looked around the empty room. "Of course, no one knows! I am the only one here!" I started to cry. "What the hell am I still doing this for? Everyone is dead. I haven't found a single survivor in all the towns I explored. The radio signal hasn't received anything. What did I do to deserve this? All the world died in the explosions, yet here I am, alive but still dead. If there is anybody out there, anybody listening, God, or whatever the hell is out there, can you please tell me why you kept me alive? I should have died in the bombs with everyone else—a corpse on the road of destruction, like so many I see. Yet here I am left to suffer this existence. There is no one coming. There is no more hope. I don't know...." I passed out on the chair shortly after, unsure of it all.

I got out of my shelter after waking to check my surroundings for the night. I do this as a precaution in case of any wild animals around me. I want to make sure that I am alone when I sleep. As I walked around the settlement, gun in hand, I saw a light I didn't recognize before, so I decided to check it out. I went back inside, grabbed my equipment of limited medical supplies and larger guns, and headed out to examine this strange light.

Many times before, I have had experiences like this one; on a late-night patrol, I think I see something, and there is never anything there. The light is of a lamp that is still on for some reason, or it is a reflection from the moon to an item on the ground. It is never anything, really.

By the light was a tent that I did not recall seeing in my travels. I wrote it off as poor surveying on my part and continued on. When faced with a situation like this, my first instinct is to kill any creatures by the light. That is what the apocalypse does to you; it makes you a trigger-happy paranoid asshole where behind every corner could be a wolf or, worse. I have seen too many beasts and animals that the sight of a human would scare me. The person I see next may be a ghost, for my mind is deteriorating sooner than I can tell you these words.

When I approached within a few feet of the light, I came across a fat man rocking back and forth on a chair, staring into the distance. He must have seen me walk up, for he didn't have any weapons on his side. "Well, look what the cat dragged in. You look like a fucker, Sargeant Pepper. Ha. Ha. What can I help you with today, my friend?"

"What is this?" I asked.

His large neck turned towards his home. "They call these things tents. You normally sleep in them. They are a pain in the ass to put up, though."

"I mean, why is it in the middle of nowhere."

"Yeah, so…. Do you have a problem with nowhere?"

The question caught me off guard. "Well, no."

"Don't judge a place until you have been there. You just got to the middle of nowhere and are telling me that my tent shouldn't be here. Now, my friend, I know you don't mean that. Nowhere is quite the place to be for me. I enjoy the alone time."

"I'm sorry; I am sure that you meant to put the tent here," I said, confused and ready to pull the trigger on this man. If he were to do anything to me, no one would know.

"Of course. I did, my friend. Would you like to come inside?" The large man got up from his chair and opened up the tent.

"What for?" I asked.

"It's late out, and the night is going to make the air cold. If you don't want to keep my company, at least come inside to warm up a bit, my friend."

"Okay. I will come inside to warm up for a moment," I answered and followed him inside as he spoke of supplies.

"Yes, my friend, I have all you need in this world. Guns, ammunition, medical supplies, food. I even know a place where you can have some fun if you catch my drift." He winked at me as if I would be entertained by a form of entertainment I hadn't known since before the bombs went off. How can anyone have fun with someone when there is no one around?

I didn't trust this man, so I knew that I would eventually have to treat him like the many animals before me. I would kill him and the threat he was. I wouldn't allow myself to be fooled.

"Sit, my friend. Go ahead. Sit." He instructed me, seeing that I was not comfortable in this small space with a large man.

The setup was what you would expect from a post-apocalyptic tent store in that it wasn't much of a setup at all. Only a few rounds of bullets and some random medical supplies were on a small table in the middle of the tiny tent.

"I thought you said that you had plenty of stuff." I sat down on a large chair in the corner.

"I do in the back. Ah, you got my good chair. I normally sit there, but for a friend, I'll let it slide. Just don't break it. Ha Ha."

"The back of where?" I looked at the entrance to the tent, which was the only way in and out.

"The tent. There is another whole part for the extra stuff. What you see on the table are only displays."

I could tell that this charlatan was trying to fool my eager eyes and deceive me with his pathetic stock. He'd overcharge me for some useless item. I have seen men like him before; they must be put down and stopped.

"I'm about to make myself some food if you want. I, of course, would have to charge you, but I can give you a discount, my friend, as you seem like a gentle guy."

I pulled my handgun out and started to fire. Six shots to the head of the merchant, and yet, when I stopped firing, he still sat where he was as if the bullets never went off. "Wow. That is quite a shot you got there. Good aim, my friend. All headshots. I am impressed."

The large man got up and stood by his pan on the oven he had in this tent. "Let's see what is on the menu tonight. There is random meat from down the river. Random meat from down the road. Or a mix of the two." He turned to me. "I love it when I have choices."

I figured that my handgun must have made a mistake, and the stranger about to cook some food was mocking my poor accuracy, so I made the logical decision and fired my sub-machine gun at him until there were no more bullets.

He felt nothing and continued to cook his meal of random meats as if the gun never went off. "You better not fire too much; you will run out of bullets, my friend. We don't want that to happen. Although that would mean you'd have to buy more from me. Haha. Did I tell you about the time that I almost burned this place down? Yes. I was trying to flip the meat I was cooking up in the air and catch it. Hey, I thought it looked cool. But then the fire from the oven got too big, and a fire started. Ha. I love cooking. It's an experiment with food." He used his wooden spatula to mix around the meat he had in the pan. "I'd offer you different drinks, but all we have is beer, which is really not that big of a problem when you think of it. In dark times like these, where all the world is miserable and sad, one needs a little bit of alcohol to sustain their sanity." He looked over at me. "Not too much, though. We want to keep that head of ours, now, don't we?"

I sat there listening to this man, and I didn't know what was happening, and I felt that I had no choice left but to go all out on this stranger who was invulnerable to bullets. I took out my rocket launcher, took a few steps to the front of the tent, and fired my only rocket. I knew I got the son of a bitch. His life was over. He would be nothing but bones and blood at this point. I even hurt myself in the explosion as I got kicked back a few feet. I got up from the ground, ready to see the body of my victim.

I was wrong. He stood making his food once more, only slightly glancing over at me as I struggled to walk over to him. "Boy, you better watch out how close you get to that, my friend. We don't want you hurting yourself. The food is still looking good, though."

He put a plate of food and a can of beer before me as I struggled to sit back down in the large chair. "Here, my friend. This one is on the house. I figure you are going to have to buy back those bullets you used, so I won't charge you for this meal."

"Thanks." I grabbed the meal. "What is it?"

"Cooked meat. I won't tell you what animal cause I don't want to ruin your appetite. So, about those supplies? What can I get for you?"

I answered, dejected by the still-living merchant. "Ammo and medical supplies."

"Coming right up." The stranger put his plate of meat on the bed he was sitting on, left his can of beer on the ground beside the bed, and left the tent. In a few moments, he came back with a box of stuff that he threw on the ground. "Here you go, my friend, plenty of ammo for your guns, medical supplies to cover those bumps and bruises you have, and I threw in a shotgun free of charge. I noticed you don't have one, and you may need one somewhere in your adventures." I gave him the money for the purchase. "You can stay to sit and eat your meal if you want."

"Thanks." I ate what I could of the unidentified meat and drank as much of the beer as possible. "So, are you going to tell me why you didn't die from the times I tried to kill you?"

He continued on with his meal. "Nah. That would ruin the fun, don't you think? Know this, my friend: I am here to help you survive out there. I am not trying to hurt you or anything like that."

"You're not even going to give me a hint."

"Nah. I'll let you think about it. *Why did that guy in the tent not die when I tried to kill him? I shot him with bullets and a rocket, and he is still standing. Is he a ghost? Am I hallucinating?*" He winked at me as if he knew something I didn't. He then got up and took my plate and can. "I'll then let you wonder where I went to get those supplies for you. Haha."

I didn't realize that conundrum until he mentioned it. Where did he go to get those supplies? There was nothing outside when I walked in. What the hell is going on here?

Before I could ask, the merchant sat down once more and stared at me as if he expected me to leave. "Well, my friend, that seems to complete the transaction."

I avoided any questioning and put my new shotgun on my back, with no more answers than when I arrived. I put the ammo and supplies in the various pockets, and I stood up and headed for the exit, which was also the entrance.

Before I could leave, the merchant said to me, "Good luck out there, my friend. Just remember that if you kill everyone in the world, there won't be anyone left to live with."

I went back to my home that night and slept it all off, seeing it as nothing more than a dream. In the morning, I woke up, and to my luck, I fixed the radio signal, yet I didn't receive anything. Curious as to why the stranger that I met last night didn't have one, I headed to the place where I was the night before, to the tent where I tried to murder a merchant but failed. To my surprise, nothing was there. No tent, no lamp. It was all gone.

What happened last night? I asked myself as I went back home, trying to understand what I went through. How could he move all that stuff so quickly? He had no horse to travel with him. He had no caravan. Am I expected to believe that a man much larger than myself, who could barely walk when I spoke to him, moved more equipment than I could carry in only a few hours of seeing him?

I convinced myself it was all a dream and that I had nothing to worry about. I went to turn on the radio to see if I could contact anyone when I saw a weapon that I had never owned before. "A shotgun?" I asked aloud. "That is going to be harder to explain."

Mr. Evil and the Tennis Rackets

Mr. Evil and the Tennis Rackets

We start the scene with a skinny bald man standing by the counter, staring at his empty fridge. "I swear I thought we got more milk. And no creamer." He looked at the coffee he had already made on the counter. "Damn." He closed the fridge. He opened the fridge. He closed the fridge again. He opened the fridge. He closed the fridge. He walked over to the two men sitting. After a few steps, he walked back over to the fridge and opened it. He poured the last of the milk into the coffee and walked over to the men sitting.

The two-time travelers Brian and Vinny were tied down to the chairs by rope and are owners of the most sophisticated time machine around. Not that there are that many time machines to go around. The last I checked, you can't buy them online. But you get the idea. The two men travel time-fighting against those who seek to hurt and cause pain to any in the past or future. They have battled kings from the past kingdoms and knights of the future. This time, the two heroes who know how to handle themselves in the face of danger will surely get out of this situation.

Vinny, the smaller of the two with a more stout frame, is the brains of the operation, for he invented the time-traveling machine with its sleek design and two-seat setup. Brian, the larger of the two in weight and hair length, is more of the brute, fighting any in their way with any weapon he can find. An adversary like the one they face now, Mr. Evil, was no match for our great heroes.

"You'll never get away with this!" Vinny called out to the villain, who was sipping his coffee.

"Oh, so now it is a crime to be the last one to use milk? We are all out of creamer, you know!"

"He means about stealing the time machine!"

"Oh…. That. Yeah. No. You'll be dead before I even get to my first spot."

"You are evil for doing this!" Vinny called out, never imagining his machine would get into the hands of a villain whose sole purpose is to destroy history itself. The inventor has come across many bad men in his travels, but they were all in the era he lived in; none of them stole his invention with the intention of traveling time.

"What part of me being evil, don't you get? Do you want me to spell it out for you?" The madman then put down his cup of coffee and, grabbed a marker and whiteboard, and proceeded to write on it. "E is for…."

"Evil?" Brian interrupted.

Mr. Evil snapped at him. "No! Hey! Who is the one with the whiteboard? Hmm? Is it you? Or is it me? Be quiet!" He continued his explanation. "As I was saying before, I got rudely interrupted; honestly, it's called manners; they are not that hard. It doesn't cost you anything to have some courtesy." He wrote out the letters as he spoke." E is for Everything." He turned to the tied hostages. "Which is what I am evil towards. V is for Villain, which is what I am. I is for… well, I don't have anything for I yet. And L is for Love because I love being evil. Did you get all of that?"

The whiteboard read:

E is for EVERYTHING.

V is for VILLIAN.

I

L is for LOVE.

"Did you make a chart just for this situation?" Brian turned to his fellow hero, confident that he was stronger than the guards by the door. "That is a weird thing to make a chart for."

"It isn't really a complete chart. He has nothing for I," Vinny responded with the same arrogance.

"Yeah, and he picked the wrong word for E."

"He may be evil but not very well thought out."

"Yeah. It's only four letters. How hard can it be to come up with a word for four letters?"

Mr. Evil zoned out as the heroes continued their back and forth. He didn't like these heroes. He didn't know these heroes. He only wanted their invention. This other dialogue seemed pointless to the villain.

"I is a pretty frequent letter."

"And E is a vowel."

"Yet this guy couldn't come up with a word for them."

"Imagine if he had a letter like X on that board."

"He'd relate his ways to x-rays somehow."

"Or xylophones."

"I never cared much for that instrument. It's only known for being the instrument that starts with x."

"Have you ever played it?"

"No. I still don't like it."

"You have to try it before you like it."

"Since when?"

Mr. Evil butted in, tired of the conversation of his hostages. "Are you two done with the witty banter? Hmm? Are you through? Cause the last I checked; I was explaining to you what evil means because someone here is too stupid to know what it means. Maybe I should check with everyone in the room. Say, guards, do you know what evil means?" They nodded their heads. "They know. Say sharks in my shark tank, do you know what evil means?" They nodded in agreement. "They know what evil means." He pointed towards himself. "I know what evil means. That only leaves you, two imbeciles, not knowing what evil is while talking to an evil man in his evil house, as his evil guards and evil sharks all know what evil is." He walked away from the heroes towards the whiteboard. "So let's review, shall we? E is for Everything. V is for Villain. I is for, well I don't have anything for that yet. And L is for Love. Got it?"

"How about you say I is for I, you know because it could be all about you?"

"Oh, that's not bad." The time machine thief responded. "The I can have a few meanings then."

"You could make I indestructible on how evil people always act that way." The one hostage suggested.

"Hmm…. Not bad."

A voice message on the phone screen popped up. "Sir, there is a package for you."

"Yeah. I am interrogating those guys whose time machine I stole. Remember how I said last week I would steal it? You said it would be better if I asked businessmen about modern slavery. How can I pay people but still make them my slaves?" He turned to his hostages. "Turns out that slavery is not as dead as you would think." He spoke back into the speaker." Anyway, the torture is going really great in here." He then faked being a torture victim. "Oh, no. That hurts. Stop, please! No more!" He talked back to the speaker in his normal voice. "Yeah, I don't think either of these guys can handle this torture. Oh yeah, this is the best torture I have ever given."

Someone opened up the door and walked in. "Here it is." It was the same woman who was on the phone, Shelly, the wife of Mr. Evil and long-time companion. Ever since the two were youngsters, they dreamt of taking over the world, nuking a city or two, causing a worldwide depression. Most couples dream of a house and some kids, but those were never in their plans. The two spent their honeymoon buying bombs from one country while convincing their allies that they were peaceful. Their villainous ways made the two a very happy couple, happier than sane couples.

"Shelly! Why the hell didn't you say you were right outside? Here I am, looking like a freaking idiot making weird torture noises, and you were there the whole time."

"The new shirts are in," Shelly said in her always stern voice.

"Oh boy!" He ran to open the boxes as he spoke to the hostages. "One of my assistants had the idea of commercializing evil with merchandise. At first, I was against the idea because commercializing evil just seemed wrong to me. It really takes away from the pureness of evil. But then I realized that I can spread evil with merchandise."

"By making t-shirts?" Vinny asked, still tied up and not moving.

"Yes. Also, coffee mugs." The two villains opened the boxes.

He showed the three shirts to his hostages. "This one says *Evil*." He picked up a second one." This one says *I am with Mr. Evil*. I figure I might as well put my name on one." Shelly held up the third t-shirt." Oh, this one is a bunch of tennis rackets. Someone on my team came up with the image, and I thought it looked cool."

"You play tennis?" Vinny asked.

"Do you not listen? No. I don't play tennis. Someone on my team does, and I thought this image would be nice on a t-shirt. Not evil, but still nice."

"Kindness and evil is a very dangerous combination," Shelly remarked, trying to organize the boxes.

"You tell 'em, Shell." The husband agreed with his wife.

"We gain the trust of people by presenting ourselves as good-hearted moral individuals, enabling us to get close to them, and that makes it easier to manipulate those who originally trusted us because we have access to the information we can use against them."

"The perfect one-two punch: Trust and betray." Mr. Evil added.

"What are you going to do with the time machine?" Vinny asked.

"You know not everything is about you, Mr. Ego?" The coffee-drinking villain rebutted the hero's question." Sure, I stole your time machine, but do you think that is all I am doing with my time?"

"No. You clearly play tennis and make t-shirts in your spare time." Brian remarked.

"Heroes are so annoying, pretending like they should be told every little detail of the villain's plans. Do I ask you what you are going to do to try to escape? No. I have some respect for you, that's why."

"Respect is so hard to come by these days," Shelly added.

"The plague of our times." Mr. Evil said. "Well, aside from that actual plague we started in Africa."

"Also, the media is quite the plague too, infecting minds more than the body. If you can infect the mind, you can control the body." Shelly commented.

"So true, Shell, so true."

The two villains continued to clean up their boxes and shirts as the two hostages sat in silence. They both carried what they could to another side of the room.

After a few trips with the packages, Mr. Evil noticed the two hostages staring at him. "Oh, I'm sorry. Did you want me to actually tell you my plan? Sure, me and my wife have a side business we are trying to start but don't worry, let me spend some time talking about what you want to talk about."

"You should have tortured these men," Shelly said.

"I'm starting to think that too."

Shelly directed her words to the hostages, "He is going to go back in time to kill all the great Halloween writers."

"What! You're a monster!"

"No. I'm Evil. What part of that are you two not getting? Do I have to show you the whiteboard again?"

"You can't go back in time and kill those people. That will eliminate Halloween."Vinny called out.

"Ah... yeah. Good job figuring that one out." Mr. Evil said.

"You should go back in time and kill Baby Hitler," Brian remarked.

Mr. Evil started to laugh. "You want me, the man who has evil in his name, to go back in time to kill Hitler, the evilest man who ever lived?" He looked at Shelly. "I swear I didn't even torture them yet."

"Could have fooled me." She said.

"You can't just go back in time and eliminate Halloween," Brian stated.

"Oh... I can't? Shelly, do I have a time machine now?"

"Yes."

"And with that time machine, can I go back in time?"

"Yes, you can."

"And have I killed people before?"

"Yes."

"Seems to me that this whole thing is not really out of my league. You can't really say that I am acting unreasonably here, can you, Shelly?"

"No. Not at all."

"You're sick!" The hero yelled at the villain.

"You say potato; I say potatoe. You say Halloween; I say I am going back in time to kill everything about it. Feels like the same thing to me."

"They are practically synonyms," Shelly said.

Mr. Evil walked over to the time machine. "Say, are there keys to this thing? Is there a button? I swear time machines are such a pain in the ass. Every freaking guy has to invent his own design. Shelly, remind me when we get back to kill the man who invented the time machine. Freaking moron." He opened the door to the machine. "Okay, well, this was fun. Oh, who am I kidding? This was boring. You guys aren't very good heroes. You know, the last guy I captured at least got into a fight with my guards, but you guys haven't even gotten out of the rope yet. I am excited to go to the past and kill all those who made Halloween. Who is the first guy on my list, Shelly?"

"Washington Irving."

"Great. I feel like I should kill him with a pumpkin. What do you guys think? Too cliché?"

"You won't get away with this!" Brian yelled.

"Oh, give it a rest, will you?" He spoke to his companion. "You know, Shelly, I think I will start off by killing Shakespeare. Is he a Halloween writer?"

"He isn't on your list."

"Well, let's add him." He turned to the heroes. "Sounds like the bard is going to not be anymore." No one laughed. "What? Not funny? Tough crowd."

"Sir, you have to kill them before we go." Shelly reminded Mr. Evil as the two sat in the time machine.

"Right. Thanks, Shell." He jumped out of his seat towards the heroes, who had not attempted to escape yet.

"I am in a good mood, so I will let you two decide on how you will die. Sharks. "He pointed to the sharks in the tank. 'Or headshot." He pulled out a gun from his hip pocket.

"When we get out of here, you will regret your decision!" Brian yelled once more.

Without hesitation, he pointed the gun at the protester and shot him in the head, killing him instantly. "Eh. I changed my mind. I am going to just kill you both. I hate in stories when villains give this long speech only to have the hero break free. Shelly, this one is for the sharks."

Shelly called over a few bodyguards who threw Vinny, still tied, into the shark tank. The creatures then devoured him.

Mr. Evil and Shelly stood motionless as they waited for the victim to get fully eaten. Neither acknowledged his cries for help.

"I'm thinking we have Chinese food when we get back. What do you think?" Mr. Evil suggested.

"I could go for some egg rolls."

"Yeah, you know I don't like how they don't give us any chocolate fortune cookies anymore. I really liked those."

"They aren't real fortune cookies. There isn't some Asian man coming up with all of those lines. They are made in a factory."

"Still. I like them."

'We should get dumplings too."

"Yeah, but do we have to get the vegetarian ones? Those are gross."

"I eat them."

"If we get dumplings, we have to get beef and vegetarian."

"That works."

Mr. Evil looked over at the shark tank that was now filled with blood. "Oh, I guess he is dead. We can go." They headed over to the machine. "I don't think they took me seriously when I told them I was evil. Eh, whatever." The couple got into the time machine, ready to cause havoc. "Shelly set the time period for Shakespearean time. We have a bard to kill."

"I think you mean a whole holiday."

"Yes. Yes. I do."

Why I Want To

Why I Want To

Before this book was conceived, with whatever initial purpose I set out with, before this story was finished, and before I even wrote any short stories laid down in this collection, I applied for multiple jobs in show business. A short story collection was not on my mind, nor was it even poetry. What were the jobs exactly? If my memory doesn't fade me, they were more along the lines of television writing than anything you will read in this collection. I felt at the time in my life, that was a viable route for me for two reasons. First, I had no professional experience in any writing venue, and I had nothing to lose by submitting for the job. Any gain was a good gain for me. When you have nothing to lose, you are more willing to take risks. Secondly, I felt that I had a skill tailored to the specific writing built on character interaction. I still feel I have an unusual ability to project dialogue quite naturally among individuals. I cannot tell you where this came from, for no one in my family is a writer and is not adept at screenplays. The most my family can tell you about writing is the latest book they have read from a reader's perspective. There are even times when I see them and we are talking, when I remind them that I am viewing the topic from a writer's take on it, not just from an observant person's. I have never taken any acting classes in my life either, which I am sure one would assume I had some experience in if I were to go into a medium where characters interacting is the entire appeal. My best guess is that my years of television watching various cartoons and sitcoms where dialogue is king, combined with my education as a 21st-century student and my own observational outlook, led to the creation of a skill most have a hard time mastering. Even to this day, I'm unsure how writers have a hard time writing characters speaking. I am with people all the time, and they speak. (some too much) Do we not all speak, just as a natural way of our own existence here? Words are spoken by the radio DJ to wake you up in the morning on your way to work, by your favorite band as the lead singer belts out the chorus, and by a waiter trying to get your order right to everyone in between. Everywhere there are spoken words. You can't name a place with people that have no words. What is the challenge of expressing some of these frequent words in a format and pattern that a stranger can comprehend? It is not like we are in a silent, mute world, and I am the only one with a voice and words bringing down my stories like Moses from Mt. Sinai. I give you words! This leads to the logical paradox: how can one teach the words they never knew?

Somewhere along the line, someone had to be taught the words, but who then taught that person? In fact, you could probably make the claim that the world is too loud, full of noises from vibrating phones that play incoherent music and explosions from action movies. When we are not being brainwashed by the sights of the technology we care for more than a child, the sounds of the world corrupt our mind and place in it by not allowing us any time to gather our thoughts. The world has become so loud that silence is disruptive.

Go to a room once and, turn off everything and just sit there and hear nothing around you. If you are like most, you won't be able to last much more than a few moments with silence, as we need to be given sounds, for without it, we are left with the one thing we are afraid of the most, ourselves. Noise is so much a part of us that without it we become confused and lost for what to do.

Sometimes, we find it hard to shut up. Most that you hear speak many words, but say nothing. The words are hollower than a cube, only being said for something must be said, but nothing to be repeated. I am sure that if you are like me, you can name a person whose characteristic is that they talk too much. They may not mean anything by it or even know that they do it, but they are the type of person that you can leave the room, go get yourself a cup of coffee, and then come back, and they will continue right on as though you never left. These people don't speak to have exchanges in opinions or ideas, but so that they can do something.

Talking is a one-person act for these people. In a world full of noise, it is only natural that we produce these types of people.

Getting back into the job search, the job applications I applied for online were sketchy as I look back on them today. They very well could have been a scam of a clever computer geek who tried to pull one over on any naïve desperate person like myself. They would present themselves as legitimate until the moment came for me to give details about myself, and then they would use that same information, which is vital to my identity, to buy something online with my money. (The great irony with this is that I have no money for them to steal anyway. I once had a scammer try to steal 800 dollars from my checking account, which only has 500 dollars in it)

Why I ever thought a stranger, whom I never had an interview or even picture of, would pay me, an unknown, unclaimed nobody, to write an episode about an idea I came up with because they were impressed by an essay I wrote is beyond me. I will blame that one on my youthful naivety, believing that luck and fortune were not only in this world but were actively on my side. Kids seem to think that the world is at their knees and that even when wrong is committed, they are in the right. I was no different at that age.

That was the other thing with these applications; I had to convince them I was good at, well, this. You know, writing. They were very much like most I know. Full of shit, and I have to persuade them I can form a sentence as if I am a salesman trying to sell a pen. These phony jobs had an exception since they didn't want a bum sending in for the job. They will scam you and try to take every dollar you ever own, but you better make sure you are good with your English, or you are out, buddy.

There is one application, of all the ones I sent over the years, and I remember it only because of the pieces of paper I found while cleaning up the office recently. My office was quite a mess, so one morning, I decided to spend the day organizing the entire thing. There were bunches of paper on several desks in my office, and I did not know the origin of most of them. Over the course of a few years, I must have put the papers there and forget about them. The issue with organizing, at least one that I have, is the unusual paranoia I feel about throwing out an idea that I only wrote that one time on the piece of paper and then never having access to that idea ever again. This is quite a contradiction if I ever see one, as any sane man can point out. If I write down an idea that is great, then surely that idea will be in other areas of the office, but if the idea is not that great anyway, what is the harm in throwing out the paper?

Nevertheless, I still spent the entire morning going through two large piles of papers. The material in it varied as much as you would think, as it had no criteria or form. There was scam mail from money lenders, magazines that I had long unsubscribed towards for my interest faded in them, receipts of car inspection visits, computer paper with various notes about money, or directions that I was to follow, and other random lines or ideas that I jotted down and never went anywhere with.

Doing such a boring task can get to a man, as it is redundant and irritating to waste time on a task you know that needs to be completed. The office needs to be cleaned; who am I kidding about that? And yet, at that moment in time, I would have rolled my eyes at you for even suggesting such a thought. (It seems I am still a kid in some areas of life) The only solution to completing such a task is to not take all your time doing it, but piecemealing it, as you can then get to other stuff in your life, the stuff that you enjoy doing and most likely have to do. Unless you are a professional maid, it is never worth taking too much time to clean, as there are other areas of your life that you are getting paid to do. Unless you don't have a job at all, which I don't want to be the one to tell you this, but it is time to get a job, buddy. Make yourself useful and get out in the workforce.

Once I got the two piles down to one, as I threw out whatever I deemed was garbage, I put the pile back on the desk. The paper on the top of it caught my eye, as it was the very essay I am telling you about now. I can't tell you why I stopped what I was doing to read the mediocre passage, but I took a minute to look at what I forgot existed five minutes beforehand.

Unlike most stories, this one did not begin at the top of the page. Instead, there were a few lines.

Joke: I'm not having an interview with you; you're having an interview with me.

Well, I thought I was funny.

And now for something completely different.

I remembered the origin of those offbeat lines; I had to make a joke to get the job (which, if I am honest, I can't even remember). If it was anything like most, I was to get paid a small fee to work on a plot that another person had developed. I was supposed to go to the filming site on the date in the description if there was one. (Remember, I could have been being scammed the entire time, and I would not have known it until the 800 dollars were out of my account) Sometimes, I got the plot of the story and sent my resume and response blindly. Those offbeat, unrelated lines were the best I could come up with at the time, I guess. The one line was a parody of a line I heard in a movie, where the guy told everyone in prison that they were locked in with him, not the other way around. It was supposed to make the hero seem like a badass, as he is the one that is the problem, not the usual case of the other prisoners. The third line was a reference to a Monty Python scene I remember watching as a kid.

Then, underneath those lines was the title *Why I Want To Be In Show Business* along with my essay. This was the one essay that would start it all and be the beginning of my career as a screenwriter. At least, that is what it was supposed to be. Now, it is on the top of a pile of garbage.

My flamboyant high school English teacher had an answer to a philosophical question that relates to my motives for being in show business.

His name was Mr. White and he had an eccentric way about him. He was always up and about with more energy than I knew anyone could have and was the kind of guy who would jump on the desk just to get the class of half-asleep, bored students going. Mind you this was first period at 7:30 in the morning where some students had a hard enough time getting to class before the second bell.

The bell would ring, and the class would be filled with 20 or so sophomore high school students reading the assignment for the day. Most of them were in the class then, but there was always one strangler who got up late or chatted with friends in the hallway one minute too long. After his introduction, Mr. White went up on the chair like he was an athlete doing a box jump drill to improve his vertical. In his dressed clothes of a buttoned-down shirt and tie and dress pants, he leaped on the empty desk at the front of the classroom to the left of his much larger desk.

Sometimes the smaller tan desk would appear to break but it wouldn't as long as he stayed on the seat part of it, not the desk part.

As if that wasn't enough, when he was not jumping up on chairs in between whatever classic piece of literature he was teaching, like Macbeth or Beowulf, a classic that is short enough for him to teach the lesson, get through all of it, and not lose the kids, he blasted a certain type of music. (Books like David Copperfield and Moby Dick, although hailed as classics today, were not taught because the schools aren't fond of teachers spending an entire year teaching the class one book) Mr. White blasted his favorite hair metal 80's music as we would come strolling in. He sat at his computer desk back and faced us with "Welcome To The Jungle" being heard throughout the room. As we all gathered in, there were always a few parts to every song that he knew really well, and before starting, he'd sing along to it. Why did he do this? Because he felt like it, it was his class and his rules, and sometimes a man needs to sing Van Halen in the early hours of the morning for the hell of it.

Not only were his antics memorable, but his appearance too. He had a full-grown brown beard and a messed up eye, which would just stay straight the whole time while the other working eye moved. Not being a shy person Mr. White addressed his eye the first day of class before jumping around. He stood at the side of the room by the computer that finished playing the music. "Yes, I know that you all noticed my eye. But think of it like this. Now I can see you when I'm on this side of the room. You just never know when I'm looking at you." That was the kind of teacher Mr. White was, not afraid to confront the elephant in the room of his eye being a new sight for us high school students, who can barely get to class on time and remember to bring in our textbooks, as soon as the semester started and before he knew any of our names. Mr. White knew that those of us who were not fascinated by his eye were talking about it behind his back. And he was right. My friends and other groups all knew him as the teacher with the weird eye. There was always one student in the group who would say after that he was a cool teacher as if we still didn't want to talk about his eye. Something that strange can't be held back from a teenager's mind and mouth.

Also, he was good at Frisbee. The game is where two or more people throw the aptly titled item at each other. I myself always had trouble with the game since the frisbee would always go too far right or left and never straight. I would throw the item into the ground twice before giving up and allowing another student to do it for the rest of the class. Mr. White was really good at it, like throwing the Frisbee from behind his back 25 yards away from his partner good. Before that end-of-the-year party, I never knew a person could have Frisbee skills, but sure enough, he and a few other teachers were throwing the thing around the football field like it was nothing in their dressed-up clothes, too.

A lesson I remember of my eccentric English teacher is one that relates to a comment he made to me as I was in extra help for one of his classes. I must have forgotten to do some homework some day or something (the details betray me at the moment), and I was stuck in the room with him and a few other kids as we went over an English lesson, like that of subject-verb agreement, a topic that is not interesting to just about any student, now or then. I can't tell you about the help that I got from that extra help session, but I can tell you a line that Mr. White said to begin the entire thing.

"You know to be or not to be is not a strong English sentence." He didn't go any further with his thoughts on the Shakespeare line, as we got to learn about how the subject of a sentence should always agree with the verb. Despite that mention of the lines in Hamlet and my lack of even knowing the play at the time, I wondered if my teacher was even right about it. Teachers who can instill short, succinct, insightful quotes to their students give them much more than a lesson ever can. Sure, we all learn lessons because we have to, because if you stay in school long enough, you may pick up a thing or two, but the special teachers are those that leave you wondering what you learned. Ever since that day, I have wondered about that Shakespeare line because of a quick remark by my English teacher who didn't even teach me that book. One of the greatest lines in all of English is not that strong of a line, grammatically speaking.

In order to attain what little attention we all had, Mr. White had a game he would play with the class when we had time, and he would ask us relevant questions he thought we should know. "What are the names of five Beatles songs?" "Who fought in World War 2?" Stuff like that. For each answer we got right, we could ask him a question about himself. Fair enough. The guy had a messed up eye; for all we knew, he ate babies for lunch and swam with sharks. (He didn't) Once, he asked us who wrote Moby Dick. No one knew it. I came the closest to knowing it with my answer of Charles Dickens. Which, of course, was wrong since Charles Dickens did not write Moby Dick. So, I guess American education is doomed because the students in an English class don't know the name of the guy who wrote the first great American novel. The closest any of us got was naming the wrong guy altogether. That is the future of America, folks; don't be too impressed. Oh, and we didn't get any of the questions right, so the mystery of Mr. White's upbringing remained. I personally liked to view him as a guy who would climb Mount Everest and then do something crazy up there, like the dance to Thriller or something. If you are going to complete an epic quest, you need an epic celebration. I also think that Mr. White would be the guy who would run a marathon but for a cause and with a catch. Like he would run it backwards for leukemia or carry an actual cross the entire time for Jesus. Mr. White didn't just run a marathon, at least not in my mind.

During one of Mr. White's morning digressions, which happened quite a lot and were as diverse on his opinions about a recent movie he saw or the high school sports game he went to, he mentioned a time when he had to write a philosophy essay in school when he was a student. Being that all students just loved essays, no one listened to his story. It's bad enough for kids to write essays, but to have them listen to a story about writing an essay, forget about it. You might as well talk to the wall; you'll get more of a response. He boasted in his deep, powerful voice that he had taken a philosophy final and completed the assigned essay in only a short phrase. The question he had to write about was, "Why?" This is a well-known question in the field that has yet to have a definitive concrete answer due to its subjective, ambiguous nature. Now, while the other students taking the test mentioned the philosophical minds of Plato, Kant, Descartes, and any other philosopher they *could think of, all Mr. White did was write, "Why not?" He handed in his paper and left the testing area before most of the other students started their second paragraph.*

He got an A on that paper.

So when you ask me, "Why do I want to be in show business?" I have a very simple answer for you, "Why not?"

I didn't get the job. I guess my take on the life of my high school English teacher is not amusing or entertaining for some, and the jokes that I made at the beginning of the essay were not that funny.

I can't pretend like I learned anything from the rejection at the time. I didn't, and that is more about my ignorance of the situation than any post-modern meaning behind it. I never heard back from them (whoever they were), and this anecdotal essay is the only remaining proof I have of the job even existing. This was a piece that, when I wrote it, I felt I was very clever in my ending. Like I winked at the reader and gave them something to think about. Oddly enough, the most useful piece of information from the essay was not the job experience, for I told you that there was none, or my eventual development into show business, for I have long abandoned that possibility, but my teacher's response to his reasoning for his philosophical approach towards life. Why not? I guess you can apply that thinking to just about every action you ever do in life. I wish to say that is a profound statement, and that was Mr. White's lesson that took me till now to grasp it, but I doubt it. Sometimes, when I am with people and they want a reason for my actions, I simply say, "Why not?" It makes as much sense as anything else.

A Trip to the Bookstore

A Trip to the Bookstore

The pandemic changed a lot of things in many of our lives, and without giving you my entire life story as though this is a memoir, I will say one particular habit that changed for me was attending Barnes and Noble bookstore.

In the late afternoon after work, I would go to the café, buy an iced beverage, decide on whether I wanted a snack, and then relax there. Not when the pandemic happened, though. The routine changed. Cancel my order, put away my book, and give me a mask because, during the pandemic, you wouldn't find me at Barnes and Noble.

Today, for the first time in as long as I can remember, I went to the bookstore since the world is done with all the madness of the COVID-19 disease. We are no longer wearing masks and flipping out when someone doesn't wear one. This doesn't mean that the world has gone sane; it is only that we got rid of a bunch of the craziness we had during those years.

Heading to the café as soon as I entered the store was a no-brainer since I could put down my laptop and bag and sit down. My job requires me to be on my feet for hours on end, so by the time I get to find a chair for my aching legs, it is much-needed rest for me, whether I have an iced beverage or not. I always buy myself an iced beverage, and I am upset with myself when I look at the receipt because I forgot about that coupon that I received last time when I purchased a book. I say last time as if it only happened once. It happens every time I buy an iced beverage. I will not go into details of what I order pertaining to the flavor or the style because they are all the same to me. Iced coffee, iced macchiato, iced cappuccino: I feel like the cafes have made the same drinks several times, altered them only slightly, and changed their names, and they have convinced people they are different drinks. They are all iced coffees; you are not fooling me!

I do not ask for no ice in my iced beverage, even though anyone who has accepted that item as their order quickly realizes that they got ice with coffee, not coffee with ice.

This is a topic that I have discussed with many people, and we all agree that the cafes do this deliberately. "I ask for no ice when I get a soda!" One man told me as he tried to outthink the system. But, of course, I was ordering an iced coffee on my trip, so I had to get some ice in it. If I get no ice in it, then I am just getting regular coffee.

Whenever I receive the iced beverage, I often think of the missed opportunity I had to be clever, and as a writer, being clever is basically all I am good for anyway. Without cleverness, a writer is nothing more than someone with too much time on their hands and a strange outlook on the world. When the barista asks for my name, I am unoriginal, so tell them the truth. Instead, I should tell them the name of a historical figure. I could say that I am Philip the Second of Macedon or George Washington Carver. However, the idea of being controversial by inserting a name like Adolf Hitler or Joseph Stalin doesn't seem worth it to me. I am there to get an iced coffee, one that I am not even sure what it really is and that, for some reason, has too much ice; I am not particularly interested in getting a strange look by saying that I am Adolf Hitler. Plus, some may not find that funny at all. As much as the world is full of amusing ironies, and notable coincidences that make you chuckle, it also is full of morons that wouldn't know a joke if you got hit with a pie or slipped on a banana peel. You can literally show some people in this world a clown, and they would not find it funny.

The biggest problem I have at the café is the food selection. They are all really good but expensive, so I am always questioning whether I should have a brownie, some cheesecake, or a scone. The coffee is expensive the way it is, but going in all the time and getting ice with coffee and a cheesecake is too much for my wallet (and my waist). My job doesn't pay that well. Thank god the pandemic stopped people from going to cafes, or else I'd be broke from all the ice with coffee I drink and the brownies/cheesecakes/scones I consume.

In this instance, I skipped out on the snack, avoided any commotion with my controversial name selection, and didn't suggest the removal of ice in my iced coffee. I waited in line and ordered as if I had no issue with the place. Meanwhile, this was the first time I had been in the place in two years.

I thought of proposing to the barista that we have a ceremony for such an occasion. Perhaps we can have a parade, with red balloons, and there can be a guy who throws a baton in the air and pretty ladies with nice hats, all celebrating my return to the café. There can be a band that plays a bunch of uplifting music, and you can have that guy who says, "Let's get ready to…" (you know the line) (I am not sure if he is going to be next to the baton thrower or the ladies and if he is going to be stuck repeating the line for the whole parade) And there can be bagpipes, because what is a parade without bagpipes? It is nothing in my eyes but random delusional individuals prancing around as if they are celebrating something worthwhile. Yes, that is how high I put bagpipes in my parade preparation. (Don't ruin the joke by asking if the bagpipes play over or with the band, either!) You may see why I don't always joke around with people; I am sure that the barista would look at me and say, "We don't do parades." Like I didn't know that, and I am the incoherent blabbering idiot unaware of their non-parade throwing policy, not the one making the joke, to deal with an event that is insignificant to the speaker but meaningful to me. "We don't do parades." That can be the slogan for a lot of the unhappy people in the world.

Sometimes, when I sit down at the table, I get work done, such as contacting clients who I don't really want to talk to, writing articles that I don't always want to write, and other business-related matters that are as boring to you as they are to me, so I will spare you the details of each email, phone call, and invoice I look over. I find that is stuff better to do at a time I never have and is best completed by someone not called me, so in this story, I am telling you, I avoided the responsible work that could benefit myself and others in favor of a more pleasant experience.

In my previous trips to the café before the pandemic, which may or may not have included a cheesecake and/or a brownie, I wrote a few poems on multiple occasions. I cannot tell you exactly what they were about, but for some reason, I wrote a poem about Conan O'Brien and Mario Kart and another poem about the older women sitting next to me. I think Conan O'Brien was playing Mario Kart, or maybe it was an analogy I was making. It is one of those ideas that makes sense in the story, but when I say it to you here, the idea seems pretty offbeat and irrelevant, to the point that you wonder if I even had a good idea. The second poem was about older women sitting at the table next to me, discussing something that I forget now. Like the Conan/Mario Kart poem, it all made more sense when I was writing it, and when you read those poems, the unrelated topics flow for some reason. Not here, though. And yes, for those of you who are keeping track of the kinds of style in the free verse that I wrote, the poems were of my stay at the bookstore. I wasn't wandering off into another world like Dante, with Virgil on my side making remarks of the layers of Hell, and I certainly wasn't speaking in rhyme as an Irish poet does of his homeland. Instead, I wrote about being in the café. Little did I know that I wouldn't be there for a few years.

On a side note, perhaps I could say that my longing for my old days of staying at Barnes and Noble was akin to an Irish poet wishing to be in the green land of the fairy-filled, magical country. Sure, I am not rhyming about my experience here, and there were no magical creatures in the store, at least, none I could identify clearly, but I can't help but point out the longing I have for a bookstore in a pre-pandemic world, is not that much different than an older Irish poet, wishing to be back in their homeland. I wanted to be in that bookstore. Can I go back to that? How do I go back to the past without actually traveling to it? Is there a way for my dreams to become a reality before me? I wanted to sit in the Barnes and Noble café with its ice with coffee and its relaxing atmosphere before the pandemic happened, and I was forced to leave, abandoning a place where I find solitude.

Life is fascinating in that instance since you never know how the future may perceive the history you recorded during a present that was not important to you. Did Melville know he was writing one of the greatest books of all time when he sat to write Moby Dick? Did he think of the influence his book would have not only on his own field but the world? I want to think that he did, but he probably didn't and wrote the thing as he felt would help the story. When I wrote the nonsense poems, I didn't know that they would define a different era in my writing life. But I digress...

Since my mind is limited with creativity most of the time I was in the store, I would wonder about the place more than any other action. This time back was no different. I abandoned any possible great verse of blue shells and Team Cocoa in favor of aisles of paperbacks and tables of hardcovers.

I didn't walk around looking for anything. There was no book I wanted to read and was going out of my way to find. I have a large enough TBR pile; I don't need to buy any more books that I won't read. Instead, I was curious about what books people were reading. What books are on the tables that many walk by? Do I know of the author? Have I read the book? If I haven't, would I buy the book?

As I have been away from writing longer than I care to admit due to other obligations and priorities in my life, I found that I didn't follow the field as much as when I was writing. I admit there is intimidation in the field of literature that I am not sure many in the field even know about. Many readers promote books they read and love, and they feel as if they are doing others a favor by presenting such works. They are talking to other literature lovers about books; what is not to love? However, I also felt isolated from these people since they were not reading many books I would enjoy. I am not interested in what they are reading, yet they and others who follow them are talking about this book like it is the greatest thing ever. So what gives? Is literature creating a special class of readers who are pushing others to read what they are told to read, and if you don't like that book, are you judged for it? The community says it is welcoming of any and all readers, but all I ever see are readers with too much time on their hands reading books that I wouldn't want to read and then making me feel like I missed out on a great book, even though I am not sure that I did. I keep quiet on this matter, for it is not a fight worth fighting. If I am right in my assessment, I am only confronting those who wish not to see me anyway, and if I am wrong, I come across as a paranoid imbecile. I suspect more is going on here with the books being discussed, but I am not the one who will delve any more into it.

My negligence in the field is why I was picking up many books and reading the back covers... I am sorry. I misspoke there. I meant to say, "My negligence in the field is why I was picking up many books and not reading the back covers since many of them, to my surprise, didn't have any." I am being serious too. I must have picked up ten books from the tables in the middle of the store, and half of them had nothing about the book on the back, only praise from strangers and outlets that I may have heard of in passing but that their mention meant little to my wandering mind.

Contrary to what many may think, I don't go around the bookstore as a writer, comparing and seeking validation for my career. I don't imagine where my books would go or what they would look like on the book-filled shelves. *Will my next book be by the door for all to see or on the new author's shelf? How close will I be to a writer that I love, like King or Rowling?* I never think any of that. I am merely a spectator taking in the scenes, not a participant in the games. I recall a video of a writer who cried when she saw her book in the bookstore that can better illustrate my point. Tears running down my face and covering my face with my shirt to hide the salty discharge are not actions you will ever see from me when my books are in the store. I'd ignore my book altogether, and if you even noticed me and thought that I was the writer of the book, I'd deny it. "Yeah, I get mistaken for that Greg guy all the time. No worries. He is quite a handsome fellow, though." I am not crying over my book being in a bookstore. I don't care how long I spent on the book.

I don't walk around the bookstore as a clueless, mindless heathen, unclear of what I like or where I am. I, of course, have certain preferences for books that catch my eye. Readers of my work will not be surprised by my genres, but I shall include them here anyway. I enjoy poetry, although not the modern Insta-poetry, as they call it, since I prefer my poems to have more words than a few sentences. Call me old-fashioned, but I am not a man who cares much for the heartfelt, short poems that are designed as emotional triggers than any true expression of the English language. I often laugh at this poetry trend because as I try to make my poems longer in size and words, most are trying to cram together whatever they can into their two lines of high school-level vocabulary.

If I pass by, I make time to check out the philosophy and mythological parts of the bookstore. I find philosophy fascinating because although it is not always present and practical, it does stimulate my mind, which coincidentally, not much else in my life does. Philosophy as a topic scares many people, and many minds of many ages and intelligence shy away from the field for fear of not being understood, yet I can't tell you how many times I have seen people question things in this very world. People like to talk about philosophy as long as they don't think it is philosophical. Once you tell people that they are thinking like a philosopher, they will look at you like they made a mistake. "Philosophy? No, I was only presenting a question in a deep manner while evaluating other possible situations. That's not philosophy!"

Mythology intrigues me more than any other genre, not for its great tales, per se, but for its longevity. I am impressed that stories from dead civilizations have survived, so I, an amateur poet who can't decide what snack to eat at the café, can read them or at least add them to my TBR. I often find myself asking if the mythological stories are, in fact, the best stories around since they have lasted longer than many. People will still know of Biblical and Greek myths long after the current best-seller is read, assuming that the best-seller is not a myth, of course. Homer will still be read long after I am dead, just like how he was read long before I was born.

I skipped that part of the store and found myself in the area of the store that no one dared approach: the poetry section.

I must say that I felt strange staring at the poetry section of the store. My small personal bookshelf at my home seemed larger than the selection that they gave me. Poetry is doing so great, they tell me, yet how many people that I know could even name a living poet? Heck, how many could even name a dead poet? Poetry is only good for commercially successful writers to add some credentials to their resumes. If you want to sell books, don't write poetry. If you want to tell people you sell books, write poetry. Today's most popular poetry book is by a dead Greek writer about an adventure from thousands of years ago, so take that for what it's worth, for how poetry is to the modern reader. On the one hand, it is quite impressive that Homer is still the top poet. On the other hand, we are all left wondering if that means that we can ever produce a poet on that level and if we can't, why?

My indecision about the small shelf was worsened because I walked by rows and rows of books that I didn't care for to get to the section that no one else cared for. In case I am not being clear, I am talking about the over-saturation of young adult literature in the store. There were more aisles for young adult books than for philosophy, mythology, and poetry combined. I sensed that the industry was pushing for this kind of book. A young adult book, not a philosophical mythological poetry book. It seemed to me that many of the books could pass off as the same. Of course, I say this as I was passing by them, and their no synopsis back covers.

I know that there are some who find value in such stories and that my criticism of them is seen as poorly placed and misinformed, but I would be lying if I told you that I look up to any young adult books. There is the idea of addressing a book to a young adult, invalidating that book from more sophisticated conversations that adults may have, which I feel is true. I view young adult as nothing more than what pop music is in the music industry: it is the most popular, and there are even a few that I like, but I don't know if sophistication is a word that I would associate with any of those books or songs. Are the best writers really young adult fiction writers? Are the best songwriters really pop musicians? As I said, I understand if there are those who disagree with me, but I have dealt with enough kids to know that the book that the kids all like is not going to be as high-minded as the adult book.

I say this, and yet the most popular author around is a young adult author, and the best songwriters are all pop musicians, so what do I know?

Everyone is reading young adult books, listening to pop music, and having no problem with it.

That was why I thought about myself and my place in literature when I stood in the poetry section. "I don't know, Greg. Maybe you are wrong. Maybe you are outdated. Maybe… Maybe people don't want to read me, and I am out of it."

Maybe the world has moved on after the pandemic, and what I write with my interest in poetry, myths, and philosophy is not what people want. I am writing to an empty void, hoping for an answer that will never come. I am talking to a stranger who isn't even there, waiting for a response. I am writing to an audience that doesn't exist since everyone is interested in other genres, all of which I don't write.

After that profound thought, I continued on my journey around the store, putting my cup of iced coffee on the closest shelf from time to time as my hand got too cold from holding it. I came across various other books that caught my eye, none worth mentioning to you in detail, and I soon found myself back at my table. My place in literature seemed no different from when this all began.

I threw out my iced coffee and closed my laptop. I decided against eavesdropping on the old women at the table next to me since I was too tired to write a poem about how they don't like the current political nature of the world. I regretted not having a snack and smiled about being back in the bookstore. Sure, no one realized this trip to me, but I was happy to be back for a brief moment. One thing I learned from the pandemic is that people, despite themselves, figure it out. We get ourselves in trouble; we all panic about how bad it is and what happens, but we get out of it... somehow. The leaders and the ones who are supposed to know what is going on are never as resourceful as the common people, who always seem willing to go against the rules and standards to help themselves and others. I was worried that I would never be back in the bookstore again. I'd never enjoy the moment of sitting at the table, pretending to work, writing a nonsensical poem, and thinking of a funny historical figure name to give the barista (Napoleon Bonaparte would be an interesting one), But here I was... again. Somehow, we figured it out. I don't know how, but we did. People are more resourceful than we give ourselves credit.

I packed up my things to go with a grin on my face and didn't worry about my lost place in the field. I will write what I write; if people read it, then that is great, too.

I headed towards my car with one last thought that made me smile.

Thank god nobody reads me, or else I'd have to worry about selling actual books.

It was nice to be back, though.

No Resolution

No Resolution

Two co-workers sat at a table in the retail store cafeteria during their lunch. Nobody but the two were in the place that sells customers food as they take a break from shopping. After a customer is done going through the clearance section of the store, which has more than you may even realize, they can grab a bite to eat at the cafeteria before they go to buy a new pair of pants or a new ottoman chair for the living room. The cashier in this cafeteria was absent from the register, probably by the dumpster smoking his e-cigarette, the popular replacement for cigarettes that are just as deadly for the consumer and profitable for the companies, although you wouldn't know that if you saw someone do it. They feel as though the lack of smoke in the air is less dangerous. There is a joke that I can make about the smoke going to their head, but I will let that be. The food ready to pick up and go was mostly empty, with no more than a few hotdogs and fries for a customer to buy. Although the vacantness wouldn't stop someone from putting the food out. It was empty, not bad. The soda machine was just as empty as the food area, with only the Diet Coke products being full, as the regular Coke, and the other products not even restocked. If you were to get something other than that, you were getting the last one. The food's emptiness made for a clean place to eat for the workers, mostly because their presence was the most anybody had been in the place all day.

Both of the guys we meet have the same blackness under their eyes from lack of sleep and overworking, and they both are slightly overweight with a belly that is enough to flow over their waist but not big enough to stop them from moving as they wish. Whether that fat is there because of dietary problems of excessive fast food or sedentary lifestyles of excessive sitting is up for debate. It could be that they compound one another. Eating chicken sandwiches and fries leads to them sitting so much. Or do they sit so much because they are eating fast food? Both are bad habits that neither seems all that worried about solving, aside from the occasional comment about losing weight. (that won't happen) If these guys are like most, I know they will lose weight by not eating for a month, only to gain it all back when they go back to their old diet of soda and hot dogs. The only thing that got either of them through the workday was the energy drinks they had before their shift, and those are starting to wear off, and they will both need another one in an hour to get through the rest of the day. As many know, the last quarter part of a work day is the worst, as you no longer have the same energy you had when the day began, and you are only thinking about leaving. The last part of a work day is the slowest part of anyway. To make my point on their abysmal appearance clearer, I will mention that neither man has shaved their beard in any capacity for a long enough time that any person who sees them would wonder if they forgot to shave or if that is a new look they are trying. The length is not Duck Dynasty long, but it is getting there.

Pat, the more cheerful of the two, had ordered the last Coke and some breadsticks, which he had to wait 15 minutes to get. His co-worker, Mike, was more interested in ordering the story of his recent fight with another co-worker, Alice. He didn't wait to tell this one.

We pick up the conversation with Mike and his half-red face and half-grown beard, being done describing it all to Pat. "So, yeah, good thing we are on different schedules 'cause I don't think I can stand working with her. She annoys me." Mike remarked on his frustration in a way that is only acceptable when he is with Pat. "Stupid bitch."

"Don't let it bother you," Pat said as he dipped his breadsticks in the sauce.

Recently, Mike and Alice got into an argument over the integrity of their work. As many workplace fights typically go, the back and forth was over trivial matters that, when explained to an outsider, make the event appear rather pointless. You don't see the frustration in both of the people's worn-out eyes. You don't know the pain in their voices. All you hear is that two people argued over where to put some boxes. Boxes, the same item that many of us discard as soon as we see it, rather being more interested in the item in the box, than the box itself. None of us care about workers fighting, as we look down upon their menial jobs anyway. We don't mean to, but we have all picked up boxes before. It is not that hard. The fight was more than that, though, as working together is a two-way team; when one feels that the other is not participating appropriately, that individual is hurting their work, frustration shows, and an altercation begins. This often brings up inner feelings that people have towards one another but keep to themselves.

When all is fine, and no one is complaining or doing anything bad, there is no point in insulting or hurting someone, but when that person is a perceived destructive force, then a person is more than capable of insulting them with partial truths. I say partial truths, for we all have our dirty little secret that allows us to get through the job. Some of us do minor offenses like taking long lunch breaks. While others do offenses that are seen as sinful in the eyes of even those not at the job, like sleeping with your supervisor to get ahead. We are all playing the same game, but we only admit our participation in it when we are mad at each other.

Mike feels that Alice never puts back the customer service items that she is supposed to deal with (according to him). He doesn't like her, for he feels that she is given credit for being there longer than him by a few years, even though she seems not as advanced in her output as some of the newer guys. She thinks that Mike is out of line and spoke rudely to her about it and that she does put back the items when she has to (according to her). She doesn't like how Mike is a selfish worker, not interested in helping anyone but himself, and his comments about her as a worker only prove it.

Both are overworked and underpaid and when things go wrong, the customers yell at them for their own apparent stupidity. None of these details were brought up in the fight, though, for it would create a harmony that neither sought out.

I am not here to resolve that problem, only to tell you about it so you know why the one guy sitting at the table was fuming.

The two (Mike and Alice) must realize that in order to work together, they sometimes have to deal with someone that they don't really like. I am not confident this will ever happen, for I am not sure how much wisdom one can attain from the process of moving boxes. If they taught lessons, then garbage men would be on the same level as scholars.

This is one story that I am more than happy only to be the narrator and not an active character involved because I wouldn't want to be the guy that says that they have to work with assholes sometimes while being overworked and underpaid.

"You have to be okay with the current working environment we have here. We are not okay with those of questionable characters getting in the way of the growth of our company. You are a vital contributor to our team, and we want that to be the case moving forward." The company ties know their part in the game, too. They lie about things to make themselves and the company look good. They don't say the word asshole to the assholes, and they never tell the workers that they are overworked or underpaid. I guess they hope that by working with them so much and never addressing them publicly, they can avoid any confrontation about the matter.

Pat, the cooler of the two sitting at the table, doesn't allow Alice's alleged antics to bother him. Partly because he is not one to worry about such things as Mike is, being the type of guy to leave work from today for tomorrow and be okay about it. Pat works as hard as Pat thinks he should work. He doesn't go too fast or too slow. If you go too fast, they only give you more work and no more money. If you do too slow, they only hold you back and don't give you any money. Pat has learned indifference is the best solution. So when he hears about another worker not doing their job, he doesn't let it bother him. If he were to work with either of them, the asshole Mike, or the bitch Alice, he would be okay in his eyes since he would go at their speed, not having any issues. He also never worked with Alice as much as Mike, so he can't say that he can empathize with Mike's attitude completely. Mike has worked more with Alice in the past few weeks than Pat has all year. His best advice for the one at the table not eating anything was to avoid her, but that is easy for him to do since he is in a different department than Alice. Mike isn't so fortunate and will come across the worker again, probably with the same results as before, as both workers believe they are right on this meaningless argument. Their pride is going to create an uncomfortable work environment if it hasn't already. The only true solution is to remove one of them from the working area, either by firing one of them or by moving them to a different department so they don't see each other. Pat doesn't tell Mike about this solution, for he knows that his co-worker doesn't want to hear it.

Aside from impractical advice, Pat had nothing else to the conversation since he didn't really want to get involved or know how to. It was above his pay rate. The best he could tell his friend was to let it go, as he would.

"You know I really like their breadsticks. You sure you aren't hungry?" Pat asked as he continued the only meal he had that day.

"Nah. I'm good." Mike said.

Pat tried to steer the conversation away from the fight. "They opened up a new Chick-fil-A around here."

"Yeah. I saw that."

For those uninformed, Chick-fil-A is pronounced as if it is spelled Chick- Fill- Ay and I am sure that some add an "l" to that third part, pronouncing it as Chick-Fill-Lay. The oddly spelled name is home to a chicken sandwich fast food place that has been captivating the public's interest in the past year due to its delicious items and top-notch service. Ever since the opening, the place of chicken sandwiches has been packed, and interest has only grown since then, as it is the only place I know of that the drive-through is always packed, even in the late hours of the day.

"You ever have it?" Pat asked.

"Yeah. It's good, but I don't get the hype for a chicken sandwich."

"Don't say things like that. You may get hurt. Some people would give their lives for it. And once they start selling that sauce in retail stores? Forget about it."

Mike mocked an Italian gangster he saw in the movies. "Hey. Forget about it."

Pat continued, "That stuff will become like pink gold. The stores won't be able to keep it in stock."

"There is a lot of hype around it that I don't get. I mean, I like it, but I guess I don't get all the craziness around it."

"You know my cousin says she won't eat there." Pat finished up his last breadstick.

"Is that because of the Sunday thing? They aren't open on Sundays, right?"

"Yeah. She says it is for political reasons."

"So she doesn't like that they are Christians?" Mike stated.

"I mean..." Pat answered, never intending for the discussion to go any further. These two men are comfortable enough with each other that topics that many would deem inappropriate or not for the workplace are a part of their regular conversation. Where others see it as wrong talk, these men are not interested enough in the mentality of the masses to change their ways.

There have been many a time, when the two have spoken about a controversial topic. Just the other day they brought up one.

"Can I say something bad?" Mike asked his friend as Pat was looking over an invoice for a customer's order.

"Can you?" Pat looked up, not really that interested in the theory he was about to be given.

"Well, yeah, it's two words. It's not that hard to say."

"What's up? Oh, and before you say it, how bad is it? Celebrity committing sexual assault, but covering it up for years bad, or I-don't-like-who-is-running-for-president-bad."

"Which is worse?"

"The first one. It's more awkward, especially since there are some who still like the celebrity."

"Yeah, it is like that, I guess."

"Okay."

"I should say that Hill told me this, and I am only repeating it."

"That means it is 11 out of 10 and both of what I said, plus another that I haven't even mentioned."

"I think that Spanish people are the new slaves."

"New slaves?"

"Yeah. They are undocumented workers, they are not legally protected, and they are separated by their status of doing manual jobs. If you speak Spanish, we think that you are the one who should do the labor."

"Jesus Christ, dude... You gotta stop talking to Hill."

"They have no rights, are paid very little, and work until they are exhausted. If anything happens to them, then nobody will help them anyway. I am starting to get why the rich like them so much."

"You done? Do you feel better about yourself for saying this?"

"The trick to solving slavery is to not call it slavery."

"That's messed up."

"I told you it was."

"Does that make it better?"

"Doesn't it?"

Getting back to the Chik-Fil-A conversation between the two men, Mike gave his take on those not going to the chicken fast food venue. "If you are going to not like a place for its religious beliefs, don't act like it is political. It's cause they are Christians. Just be honest about it."

"You shouldn't dislike a place for their own beliefs like that, anyway."

"I wonder if she would be against them if they were a different religion? Like if they were Jews or Hindus?"

"I don't know." Pat got up and threw his garbage out in the empty can.

"It begs to question if that stuff really matters. Like does the fact that they are a Christian place affect the sandwich that you are buying? They shouldn't give you less of a sandwich because of their faith."

"It shouldn't. They should give their best food to you regardless of what they believe." Pat applied his thoughts to all places. "Or whatever service they are giving you." He sat back down.

They stopped talking to regroup from the energy drinks wearing off in the empty, unused room where no worker goes and barely keeps track of the unfilled napkins, the plastic utensils area with only spoons, and the ketchup packs that were mixed with the mustard packs. They both spoke of how a worker should give their all regardless as they sat in a room of desolation and hopelessness. In a place where any person would walk in and say, "This place is giving their best effort." Clearly.

"Plus, what if the guy who ran the place was bad." Mike clarified. "You know, like evil. Should that matter to you?"

"Yeah. What if they were Nazis? You can't support that."

"If they were Nazis, they would be NASA."

"Oh shit," Pat said of the joke made by his buddy.

"Your cousin doesn't realize that she is answering a profound philosophical question," Mike commented on the person he never met.

"I'll make sure to tell her the next time I see her."

"Or maybe she does understand what she is saying. I don't know the woman." He resolved.

In the vacant cafeteria, the oldest guy on the crew, Hill, walked in; he was responsible for bringing in the garbage carts from outside the parking lot to inside the store. He gets along with everybody, even Alice, for he talks to everybody in the same way, and nobody really takes him that seriously, for his wild rants amuse anyone around to hear them. His co-workers adore his uplifting personality, as he says hi to everyone he sees, but they all feel he is missing a screw loose in his head, so they are quick to keep their distance from him. He also says "bro" in every other sentence, which I am sure infuriates some of his acquaintances.

"Hey, bro." Hill addressed his co-workers, who sat before him.

"Oh, hey, Hill. Did you have a good new year?" Mike asked.

"Any new resolutions that you are working on?" Pat questioned half-mockingly.

"Nah, bro. Cause I see through the illusion of the New Year. Of the lies we are told of it."

"Is that so?"

"Yeah, bro. See, the people in the New Year are the same as the ones in the old year. You still you. You still you. I'm still me. One day ain't gonna change that, bro. You know?"

He went in line and picked up a hotdog and a Diet Coke as he continued to talk to them across the empty room, "See, they want you to believe that the New Year changes you. But I ain't about that life, bro. I don't do resolutions. The only resolution I have is the deception I see through."

"The Deception I See Through, that sounds like a novel." Mike pointed out, getting no response from either of the other two.

Hill paid for his food to the cashier, who was all of a sudden just there and without his e-cigarette, and continued to talk as the others started to tune him out, "Don't let the year make you make the year yourself. You know what will happen next year, my bro? The same thing. You'll sit and name a resolution that you'll have, never seeing that the only change you have to make is with yourself, not the year. One day like that shouldn't change your life."

The two younger workers have heard this type of rant from Hill before. Just last week, he told Pat that there is a conspiracy about the country's laws. "Bro, whenever there is a major law passed, they always be a shooting or something. You ever notice that? They pass a law that changes everything right when they talk about a kid shooting up a school. Cause they know that nobody is worrying about that law then. We talk. They pass. And no one knows, bro." As I said, many give Hill the time, for he could be their grandpa, but none of them take him and his absurd rants seriously. Of the two workers, Mike talks to him about his ideas, whereas Pat only listens until the old man is done talking.

Hill stepped over to the table where Mike and Pat were sitting. "Bro, open your mind and see the world for what it is, not what they want you to see. My resolution is not forgetting my own self can be better, not from a day on the calendar, though. You know? Cause then you stepping to their tune. You dancing to their beat. You doing what they want. Not seeing that the change you want is not a calendar date but from within. A ball dropping from a building shouldn't change you, bro, you know? Only you can change you."

The store manager, the least tired of the four and the best kept, then walked over to the cafeteria entrance and called over to the rambling co-worker. "Hey Hill, we got some extra carts in lot A that need to be brought inside. Mind taking them in?"

"I got you." He sipped his soda and headed for the exit.

He pointed his half-eaten hot dog at the angry co-worker. "Hear what I say, little bro. Hear what I say."

The older worker left the cafeteria to complete a task he should have done a half-hour ago.

Mike then spoke, "You ever think that Hill isn't altogether there sometimes?"

"Yeah. I stopped listening to him when he got a soda. So what are you going to do about Alice?"

"I am not sure."

"I have an idea..."

"What?"

"You can say that you understand her pain and suffering because I recently found out that she is really an alien from outer space and that sometimes, under stress, they shed. Give her some treats that should make her feel right at home."

"You think I should let it go."

"You said it yourself, she is a bitch, and bitches who don't sleep with you or are married to you are not worth getting worked up about."

Mike said nothing, seeing the point in the statement.

Pat continued, "You don't even like this job; why are you getting so upset about it?"

"I don't know."

"I am getting back to work."

"The stuff you left yesterday."

"You know it."

"You're a wise man, sir."

"I know."

Mike got up as the two started to leave the area.

"I am going to get myself a snack for the afternoon."

A Candy Bar and a Photograph

A Candy Bar and a Photograph

Mark stood in the middle of the living room, staring at the photograph of him and Johnny Notox. "Why did I pay forty dollars for this?" He asked aloud.

Johnny Notox was the lead actor in the Broadway play *Elf*. The show ran for a week despite there being much hype around it, and Johnny Notox, of no fame that any would be interested in hearing, hasn't been in a musical since. Was the man talented as an actor? He has all but left the scene of theater and is currently working with his father as a manager for a fruit market. How much talent do you think the man whose role was to play a man-child actually had? I will tell it to you straight; he had little talent. The only reason that he was given a role is because of his similarity to the star of the film *Elf*. If you didn't know any better, you would think that Johnny was the younger brother of Will Ferrell, which is exactly what the casting director for the play wanted; unfortunately, the lead star didn't tell anyone that his heart was not in it as much as when he was younger, and that he was more than likely calling it quits after the play's run.

Did the actor quit his life of show tunes and dance because the play was a complete mess with him as the star, and all anybody said when they left the theater was, why the hell wasn't Will Ferrell in the production? Or was the guy who would admit to having average acting chops, even though he went to school for such a craft, bound to leave no matter how well the play did? That is a tough call, for as I said, the only way to get in touch with this Johnny fellow is to go to a fruit market out east and then ask for his name. From what I know of the man, he may even deny any involvement in the production of the Christmas musical.

Mark, whose only involvement in the play was that of an audience member, got a photograph with Notox at the end of the second show because he felt obligated to commemorate the occasion. For when does one get to embrace the sounds of the show, the glory of the stage, the experience of a theater? That is a serious question.

Commoners, like myself, do not know much of that world; we only see the stage every so often, and even that is a lie. We pass the local theater every time we go to the mall, the market, the game, or just about anywhere else in the world. The theater of plays is not a place where the locals enjoy gathering. Locals like Mark. The same type of guy who is thrilled when the local fast-food place is giving away coupons for his favorite meal or when his favorite baseball team has a game at 1 PM on the weekends. Musicals are not for the average person for no other reason than price. Why go see something that can cost that much money when the person can go on their phone or computer and watch something for free? Mark has to save up to see a musical because if he paid it all in full, he would run out of money.

When a guy like Mark, who is smart enough to question the world around him but dumb enough to buy into all he sees, goes to a musical, there is a catch. He got a deal off of the show. He found a coupon in the newspaper that is only good for the current month. A friend gave him the tickets because they couldn't attend the show. Mark doesn't go to see musicals or plays often. Like most of us, he views it as a foreign world of talented yet strange individuals. Those in musical dance to the beat of their own drum quite literally. They wear eccentric outfits, talk in funny accents, and then parade around the stage as though they are doing something when all they are doing is following a story. There is no culture as distinct as that of theater. They make the stage their own world, and if you don't understand that mindset, you view the entire event as slightly off-putting.

Why did this man who has better things to do during the night go to see a Christmas-themed musical starring someone he never heard of up until then? Because he got a coupon. That is why. Coupons are the reason for many of life's events, especially in a time when money is king as much as any man. I am convinced that coupons started WW1, not the assassination of Franz Ferdinand. Who killed Kennedy? I suspect it was the man who did not use all of his coupons for that day. (Some are more passionate about saving than others) Why did the Jews and the Romans kill Jesus? Was it because he was breaking their laws? No coupons. Although the Gospels don't elaborate on it, I think that coupons had a place in the death of Christ. If we go back in time, we can find that many of life's most puzzling questions can be addressed with coupons. I have no proof for this, but I have nothing against this either.

"I'm an idiot," Mark explained to no one.

All the actors and actresses went to the lobby after the performance to give the fans a chance to take a photo with them. Anyone could have a picture with the actors for a price. Because apparently paying to see the show is not enough for the production, they make the spectators pay a little extra to get a picture of themselves with the star of the play, who was Johnny Notox.

Credit to Johnny Notox, in the picture, he was quite enthused and proud of the moment, with his young bright smile being the largest thing in the photo. Johnny was as proud that there were people who were interested in paying for his picture as much as his own performance in the musical, which, if you ask Mark, you'd get no answer. Mark neither remembers the musical nor much about it, as he only likes the movie version of the story, the one with Will Ferrell better, as most do.

"I didn't even like the damn thing. And what is wrong with my smile?"

Out of the shower in only a tan towel walked Susan, who normally enjoys walking around the small apartment all bare, with a towel to cover up her breasts and other lady parts. Mark says nothing of it because he has become accustomed to his girlfriend's peculiar habit. He doesn't have the nerve to ask how gravity works pertaining to her boobs. How do they keep the towel there? It is magic if Mark has ever seen it. Plus, not many sane men will object to an attractive woman voluntarily wearing fewer clothes. Most men spend their days trying to get women to take off their clothes, so men are more than willing to allow a woman to wear less because of her own prerogative. She is comfortable, and he enjoys the view. It is a win-win if I have ever seen one.

She welcomed her boyfriend after the twenty-minute shower where she went through her herbal scent hair conditioner and berry body wash. She is low on the conditioner and will have to get some within the next few days. "Hey." She sat down on the brown couch, grabbed a candy bar on the coffee table, and took a bite.

Still standing in the same spot as before, Mark lifted his filled ear up at Susan. "The show starts at seven."

The two of them are going to see the play *The Italian Dictionary*, which is about an Italian immigrant finding his way in America while learning more about his Italian roots. The score of the play is mostly classic Italian songs. Being Irish, Mark is not entirely eager to see the play. But like I said, coupons do wonders. It is incredible how the enjoyment of something goes up once the price goes down.

Susan is part Italian, and even took the course while she was in college. Her clear white skin and blondish hair would not have you guess she was part-Italian. You would guess she was quite busty (with or without the towel) but not Italian.

"What's that?" Susan reached her hand out so Mark could hand her the overpriced photograph. Forty dollars to take a picture with a stranger. And one in which Mark isn't even smiling properly.

"The photo of..." He gave her the photo. "You know."

She examined the photo but not nearly as much as Mark. She only saw two men in the picture smiling. This event was not one of family and happened before the two even met, so her interest in this photo is justifiably low.

"Wow, you spent forty dollars on this." She took another bite of the candy bar.

"Yeah." He answered, discouraged.

A distortion of Mark's face caught Susan's eye. "What's wrong with your smile?"

There are two things wrong with Mark's smile; he is ugly and there is not much of anything that he can do about it. No matter what he does to his large face, his pale skin, or his round body, Mark has been blessed with the gift of appreciating the personality that God has given him, only because the Lord skipped on the looks and money for the guy. The guy makes Shrek look attractive.

The ugly fool also doesn't know how to smile without looking like a creep. When he smiles, others in the room turn away quicker than a fighter does against Medusa because they all think that the man is a pedophile or a rapist or one of those bad things that none of us want to be. You know the words that men have lost when they are even mentioned in the list. That is what the ugly monster looks like when he is taking a picture. For a world where he is forced to smile to get by, as that trait seems as useful as any skill you learn in school, Mark has yet to learn the art of the smile. If he smiles too wide, his ugliness shows up more than bums on the subway. If he doesn't smile, he looks sadder than a kid at the doctor's office. Also, he looks like a creep, which is practically the worst thing a man can be called aside from a Nazi. Hell, I know a few guys who wouldn't mind being called a Nazi. When you are a creep, you are told that you are a monster and that if this was Frankenstein, we would all kill you if we had the possibility. Get your pitchforks out, ladies and gentlemen, because that man is a creep.

The man is ugly, bad with pictures, and stupid enough to waste forty dollars for a picture with a celebrity (if you want to call the lead actor that). How the man ever got his girl to stay around for longer than twenty minutes is a mystery no one has solved.

He walked towards the bookshelf and began to scan his library of too many how-to books and classic novels. Mark has ten new skills, as long as you never ask for a demonstration, and he has read three classics if you combine all of what he read.

"That is what I ask myself every time I look at you." After little thought, he selected to read *How To Play Guitar* and sat on the empty part of the couch. While chewing, Susan offered him her candy bar, which he rejected. She quickly had the last piece of her candy before he could change his mind.

"More for me." With a full mouth, she reasoned. "At least it was for charity."

The forty dollars supposedly wasted went to Alzheimer's patients, although neither in the couple ever looked into this promotional side of the photoshoot. What exactly does the taking of a picture of an elf have to do with a medical disease that affects seniors is a question that I am not qualified to answer. Some of life's more sophisticated are too much for even me, the writer of this story. The funds from the pictures are somehow helping the old people regain their memory, somehow. Or are the funds being used to find cures (that we don't even know about) for the old people? Something like that. Like I said, though, there are some questions in life that are best left unsolved.

"I'm glad I could help." He put the book on the table and opened a random page.

Susan caught on to his indifference. "Are you actually happy it was for charity, or are you just saying that?"

"I don't know. I don't know. "

"You should be happy about giving back."

He flipped the page.

"There's a surprise. You don't know something." She reached for another candy bar. "Don't eat so much; we're going to eat after the play."

She disagreed with his take and showed no sign of hesitation when she unwrapped the second bar. "So... You should be happy."

He muttered to himself. "Like I am with the photo."

Susan continued eating, "The more I eat here, the less I eat at the diner, and since you'll have the check..." She let him figure out the rest.

He reached for another candy bar and handed it to her. "Here."

She adjusted her towel so nothing would be revealed, got off the couch, and grabbed the remote control.

Nonchalantly, she turned on the television and spoke to herself about the problem the TV had been having. "This TV is done. We have to get a new one. Look at this." She moved the remote around in her hand. "I can't even change the channel. And I know it's not the batteries; I just changed them."

With the book in his lap now, Mark stared at Susan, hoping she had seen him out of the corner of her eye. She did but ignored him.

"Do you mind?" Mark was upset that his reading was interrupted, even though he had yet to choose a section to read.

"What? It's not like you're reading anyway."

Mark rolled his eyes and slammed the book shut. "Fine. I'm going into the kitchen!" He took himself and his book to the kitchen table for some peace and quiet.

Susan continued trying to change the channel. "You want to talk about wasting money. I bought him that book two years ago, and he still doesn't know what a chord is."

"I can hear you." There is no wall separating the kitchen from the living room.

"And you wonder why you waste stuff?" She turned to face Mark.

"Because you get distracted so easily."

"I wouldn't get distracted if certain people knew what quiet was."

She went back to watching TV. "Do you mind? I'm trying to watch my show."

The next exchanges are of the two snapping at each other, not being able to handle the other anymore.

"Why are you acting like this?"

"Acting like what?"

"You're being a pain in the ass right now."

"So are you!"

"Shut up!"

"Fuck you!"

Then, the two threw insults at each other, for they could not stand the other being even around.

"You are no good bare-ass slut, who thinks the world revolves around her. Ungrateful cocksucker who can't even suck cock. What the hell are you good for aside from causing me headaches?"

"You're a cheap piece of crap who is so stupid that even when you try to read, you forget the words. I know kids smarter than you! Examining a goddamn photo like it is a major investment in your life. You fucking loser! By the way, I looked into checking you into an asylum, but they said you were too crazy!"

"You're slow and fat, and no man in their right mind would ever want to have kids with you. Even drunk guys look at you and pass because they know you are only a mistake! You entered this world as a mistake, and you have been one ever since!"

"Please! You are the kind of guy the Nazis planned the Holocaust for. They thought they were doing everyone a favor by killing people like you, and they were right! You are a disgrace to the gene pool."

"I wished I lived in a concentration camp! It would be easier than living with you! All you do is complain, complain, complain; never once do you ask me about my day!"

Confrontations like that have occurred before and on even worse levels. No harm has been done to the relationship between them. At least nothing that both of them know of. Some might say it has helped them learn how to survive a relationship. Some may say it is the seeds of a dying relationship. The library does not have a book on that.

Instead of continuing the argument that was about much more than words, the two went their separate ways. Mark went outside on the patio and Susan went in the bedroom.

Both had tough days they did not want to speak about. And both had problems the other should know.

Outside, Mark sat and, for the first time all night, tried to understand the content in the book. It wasn't long before he put it down and grinned at Susan's comment. "I can't even read the damn notes."

He had a much bigger issue on his mind than his inadequate guitar skills and his poor financing.

In the bedroom, Susan, for the first time that night, took off her towel and put on some clothes: a large white t-shirt that used to be Mark's but is now hers and some pajama pants. She skipped on anything else, as her panties get all bunched up when she sleeps, and she has since learned to avoid that by not wearing anything down there. She examined her body as if nothing had changed from it. She didn't see anything major. Should she see something yet? She wasn't sure. She, too, had a secret she was hiding.

As she wiped the nervous sweat from her forehead a knock came from the door. Mark leaned his head in the door and saw Susan being more conscious about her body then usual. He sat on the bed with his back towards her.

"You know you're beautiful." Susan did her best to act like she wasn't going over every inch of her body in the mirror. "Why else do you think I let you walk around in just a towel? About what I said..."

"I'm sorry." She apologized with her head down.

"It's okay." He went to hug her, but she turned away.

"I'm pregnant." She said as straightforward as she could.

"Oh crap." He turned away from her.

She turned back towards him. "That wasn't the response I was hoping for."

Mark exited the room in a hurry and paced around the living room.

"I am happy. I really am." Susan followed him into the living room, and he almost knocked her over, but then he stopped pacing. "It's just..." He took a deep breath. "I got laid off today."

"Oh," Susan answered, followed by a long silence.

"Yeah."

Another long silence echoed throughout the room as the two sat on the couch.

"So now what?" Susan asked.

"I guess we're not going to the play," Mark answered.

She sat dumbfounded, "You think?"

"Wait..." Mark reasoned out the situation, bringing up information Susan had long forgotten. "I got a vasectomy three years before we met."

"Oh..."

Susan's other secret was out.

Bad Timing at the Ledge

Bad Timing at the Ledge

On an early morning, just past midnight, Mark had decided his fight for life would end. He would jump from the eighth-floor story building.

Life had failed him with her broken promises and broken dreams. Where was the great life that Mark was promised? Where was the success? Where was anything that he was told would be his?

"When you get older, the world will be yours," older folks would tell his younger self. Now, he is older and no greater, less successful, and was lied to. No more. In this world of able crooks and wicked thieves, where was he to go? Institutions are input to withhold any sense of freedom or individuality Mark had. And his fellow man spits on him when he is down.

"Easier to get to the top when this bum is out," others would say of him. He could no longer deal with the world. He was going to leave it. It's not like anyone would notice anyway. Darkness filled his heart, and jumping was his solution, his choice, the poorest choice he could make. The only decision that could be considered better (relatively speaking) was that Mark did not try to shoot himself or hang himself. He had already climbed up the eight floors but had not taken that final step forward. He still had time to reconsider.

He stood at the edge of the ledge, breathed one last breath, and said goodbye to the night, the only thing listening. "This is it! Goodbye, cruel world!"

But he didn't jump right away. He froze there. Motionless and uneasy, but still alive. Many can talk of death and destruction to themselves, and some may even convince you that they are going to do it, but when the time comes, to end yourself, to put your light out, to be no more, takes something that many don't have, and should never try to get.

"So, are you gonna do it or not?" A voice called from behind Mark that almost made him trip and fall.

"Huh? Where? Who are you?"

A well-dressed, slender man stood by the sidewall of the roof, looking on at Mark as if bored by the situation.

"I'm the guy you met at the deli a few years ago when they gave you the wrong order of bacon, egg, and cheese rather than ham, egg, and cheese. I've come to save you."

Mark said nothing, confused about what was happening.

"I'm a demon, you idiot," the figure admitted.

Mark turned back around to the street side of the edge. "So, what are you doing here?"

The demon folded his arms. "Waiting... for you to go."

"I will!" Mark shouted back at the demon. "Don't think I won't!"

The demon calmly responded, "I don't care either way. Just make it quick. The boss has been nagging me lately."

Mark prepared himself for the end. "Okay, here I go."

"You should have just shot yourself. It's easier for me that way," the demon said candidly while staring down at the ground.

"Huh?"

"If you shoot yourself, I don't have to walk all the way down there and clean you up. Heck, sometimes I shoot the guy myself, but go ahead. Go on. Don't let me stop you."

"Okay. Okay." Mark once again prepared for his end. Sweat poured down his face, and his feet were shaking slightly.

But that final step didn't move.

No matter how bad he was feeling, he couldn't do it. He has nowhere to go, for his home was taken from him years ago. He had nothing to live for, as he lost all purpose for being, but he couldn't take his own life. Perhaps an angel was holding him back, trying to tell him that he could still win, that even though all he sees is darkness, there is still some light in his life, or maybe the kid inside him was making his last stand to live, one last effort to tell his adult self that there is something worth living for in this life, because there are things in this world that make him happy, there are those that he loves and cares for. Something was holding him back.

Mark wanted to die, but he didn't want to end his life.

"Can you imagine if you jump and a major disease happens shortly after? That would be funny. You think that everyone will talk about you, but then they don't because a massive outbreak occurs, killing a bunch of people," the demon spoke out of term again. "Just get this over with already." The demon picked up the phone in his pocket and walked away from Mark.

"Yeah, I know. I am taking care of it."

Mark stood there without movement as the cold night froze his sweaty face. The longer he stood there, the more he couldn't take the last step. The goodness in him was trying to tell him to get off the ledge, to go back inside, and continue to live.

"Oh. You're still here?" The demon came back from his call.

"When I was a kid, my parents took me to the Statue of Liberty." For the first time, Mark's eyes saw some of the light in the night. "It was beautiful. I said that I would take my family there one day, too. And then to the great statue that I designed. When I was a kid, I wanted to be an architect."

"Oh, whatever. I don't care."

"I was going to design a great statue that everyone would marvel at. Now I'm jumping from a no-name building."

"How poetic."

"I loved designing statues. I loved the Eiffel Tower. I want to go there one day." Mark paused as if to acknowledge that moment would never happen if he jumped. "And don't get me started on the pyramids," Mark commented, a line he had said to many others in his life when that feature was brought up, for he could go on about it for days. The kid in Mark was winning and convincing his adult self that the enjoyment he knew then was still here. It never left. He took one deep breath as tears fell from his face. "I can't. I just can't do it." He turned to get off the ledge. "I won't let that win."

Before he could get down, the demon, tired of listening to him, stretched out a hand and pushed him off.

"No!" Mark cried, falling to his death.

"Poor bastard." The demon looked down below. He answered a phone call. "Yeah. Boss. It's done. I know. I know. I'll be right over." He put his phone back in his pocket and hurried off the roof.

Later that morning, a virus broke out across the world, killing many. No one ever mourned the loss of Mark.

The Gun on the Wall 🍺

The Gun on the Wall

Lenny walked back into the living room of his lifetime friend, Brad, with the last can of beer out of the refrigerator. There are some alcohol bottles in the study, but no one in Brad's family ever goes in that room. It has been a storage room for the past 20 years.

"Hey Brad, you're all out of beer," Lenny told his friend, who was already sitting on his large living room couch.

"How dare you say such vile things, you heartless heathen!" The fatter of the two called out.

"Eh, don't worry; Jack is on his way over with some more."

"Oh, thank god."

"What is that gun doing up on the wall?" Lenny asked.

"Huh?"

"That gun. Why on earth is there a gun on the wall?"

"I don't know." Brad had never noticed the piece in the room before.

"I know what this means."

"One of us is going to jail for looking at a gun we may or may not own."

"No. We have to shoot something with it. That is why it's up on the wall."

Lenny put his beer on the table and walked over to get a closer inspection of the gun. Being of large stature, this task was not difficult for the man.

"What? Says who?"

"Everyone knows that a gun is never just put up on a wall. You gotta grab it and shoot someone with it eventually in the story."

"That's stupid."

Lenny took the gun off the wall. "Hey, I didn't make up the rule." He pointed the gun directly at his friend. "Now, who do you want to shoot?"

"Don't shoot me!" Brad pushed the gun away from his face.

"Oh right..." He put the gun down. "I have it on safety." He pointed the firearm back at his friend.

"Not me!" Brad pushed the gun away a second time.

"Alright, sorry." Lenny pulled the piece away from his friend's face." My god, stop making such a big deal of this. It's like you don't want to get shot."

"I don't."

"I am going to put the gun down on the table; that way, neither of us will get hurt." He put the gun on the table beside the extra plastic village house that couldn't fit with the kitchen table and two used plates from the lunch that Brad had eaten before his friend arrived.

"That's better," Brad said, relieved he would no longer look down the barrel.

Lenny took a seat on the one-person sofa piece as Brad sat on the large couch in the middle of the room. They both stared at the gun they really wanted to shoot.

"Now, to who we will shoot."

"I have a neighbor I don't like that we could shoot."

"The one next door?"

"No. The other one."

"The one in the yellow house?"

"No. The other one."

"Oh, just tell me! Which neighbor do you hate?"

"Hmmm…. I hate all my neighbors."

"We don't have the bullets for that. How about your crazy aunt?" Lenny suggested.

"No. She is in Florida; too far."

"Crazy uncle?"

"He's already dead."

"Boy, no wonder wars take so long. Who knew it would be so difficult when deciding on who to kill?"

"Maybe we should go with someone we don't know."

"Like the president?"

"Nah. Too much work."

"Your boss?"

"No. I have to work."

"That jackass from high school you saw last week."

"That was last year, and he moved to Florida."

Lenny got up from his seat. "Why does everyone move to Florida?"

"I don't know; the weather?"

The third friend of the crew, Jack, entered the house with the pack of beer. Jack was the slightest in frame of the three men and although could outdrink them both, looks too think to appear as though he even likes beer. "Oh hey guys, what's going on?"

"We are deciding on who to shoot with this gun?" Lenny informed his pal.

"Oh, ok. I'm going put these in the fridge."

"Can you bring one in for me too?"

The friend carrying the beer came back into the room with a can for him and the house host. "So why are you shooting someone again?"

"Lenny found this gun on the wall, and that is the rule."

Lenny elaborated on the rule. 'According to the literary principle of Chekhov's gun, "If in the first act, you have hung a pistol on the wall, then in the following one it should be fired. Otherwise, don't put it there."

"Yeah, but that isn't a real rule. You don't have to follow it. Kind of like how the hero doesn't always save the day and get the girl."

Brad reacted to this sad news of his favorite stories. "He doesn't? Hollywood has lied to me again with its spectacular scenes and sexy sirens!"

From the other side of the room is the child of Brad scraping the paint of a village house piece with a scissor. He stopped ruining his mom's collection and spoke up to his father. "Why don't you do us all a favor and shoot yourself?"

"Haha! I love your kid." Jack said of his friend's child.

"Yeah, but you know, once he reaches a certain age, his attitude will be annoying," Lenny said.

"Oh, of course. But for now. I like him."

Brad addressed his kid. "Jacob, that is very mean to say to someone. You never know what the person is feeling on the inside. You should encourage them to live, not die."

"But that's not fun."

The kid's father spoke up, "It's not about fun."

"Then what is it about?"

"Uhhh. guys?" He looked at his friends for help teaching his kid.

They both shrugged their shoulders as if the concept was too advanced for them.

"Freedom?"

"God?"

Brad ignored them and directed his focus on his kid, "It's about being kind to someone that you don't know."

"But I do know you. That's why I said it."

"Oh my god." He went back to sit on the large couch next to Jack. "Don't you have kid stuff to do? Like climb a tree house or go to the arcade or something?"

"We don't have a treehouse, and arcades aren't really a thing anymore."

"Oh right... Can't you do something stupid that I have to pretend like I didn't know about as your mother tries to defend your fleeting innocence?"

Jack directed his attention to the kid, "You should use that excuse as long as you can because once you are a teenager, people won't think it's cute."

Lenny, the gun enthusiast friend, spoke up, "Yeah. Go smoke or drink beer or start an addiction that you'll regret when you are older."

Jack finished that thought, "And at that point, it won't be about how much fun you can have with the vice, but all the fun the vice has taken from you. Good times."

"Uh... ok." The kid began to walk out, but before he left, he turned around to his father, "Does this mean that you are not shooting yourself?"

The father sat motionless, not even changing his line of vision. "No."

"Man, you really know how to ruin a kid's day." The child left the room.

All three of them now sat comfortably on the pieces of furniture as Jack spoke to the other two, "Hey, I was thinking that this rule is not real because what did they do before guns? You know they weren't around forever."

The three didn't say anything for a minute, since up until then, they thought guns existed for all of time.

After the prolonged silence, Lenny asked, "So how much do swords go these days?"

"We're not buying a sword!" Brad stopped his friend's crazy idea.

Jack said, "Look, we should give this gun-shooting thing a break and talk about something else."

"Fine, but if we get to the third act, and that gun is still there, I am shooting someone."

"So, what do you want to talk about?" Brad asked.

"Uh… what shoe do you guys put on first? The left or the right? I always put my left one on first. I think it means I'm patient or that I'm impatient. One of the two."

"Oh, come on. That is so boring! What are we going to talk about next? The benefits of toilet paper roll facing up."
Brad rolled his eyes at his face's bland conversation topic.

Jack then crumbled up a piece of paper while the others weren't looking that read "WHY UP IS BETTER" "No. No. That would be stupid." He gathered himself in his seat next to the host. "How about we talk about our new year's resolutions?"

"Jack, you know that they are pointless because no one will keep them."

"Yeah... We could shoot the president. That would be fun."

"No, we already discussed this," Lenny said as he finished his can of beer.

"What? He isn't in Florida. It's fine."

"So it's settled we are going to shoot the president." Brad clarified.

The three got up with Lenny carrying the gun and headed for the front door. Jack asked the question the two already wondered, "Hey, do you guys notice that everyone moves to Florida? What is that about?"

"Must be the weather," Brad said.

Brad's wife opened the door before the three men could leave the house. "Oh hey, honey. Where are you guys going?"

"To shoot the president."

"Oh, ok.... Wait, just so we are clear, you aren't actually doing that, right?"

Jack said, "No. We are probably going to drive down to the bar and then drink until dinner time."

"Come on, sweety. I would never shoot the president. I love my country of red, white, and blue and the freedom it gives me." Brad told her about his passion for the only country he had ever lived in.

"Yeah, plus that is way too much work," Lenny said, explaining the real reason the act would not be done.

"Ok. Have fun."

"Maybe we can shoot the bartender while we are there!" Jack called out as Lenny followed behind him.

"Oh yeah!"

"Wait, but he is our friend," Brad told them about to close the door behind him.

"Oh, right."

Just as the father was about to leave the house, his son asked his mother about her approval. "Hey, Mom, why did you allow Dad to take that gun outside of the house?"

She spoke so only the boy could hear her. "That is a replica gun that is broken and doesn't have any ammo. It can't hurt anyone." She saw the bottle of alcohol in the boy's hand. "Why do you have that?"

"Dad said he wanted me to start an addiction that will ruin my life."

The wife stared at the husband before he left. He stopped and spoke softly to his son, "Oh, silly boy. I said to never drink because that could ruin your life."

"Like yours?"

"Give me that bottle. And promise me you'll never drink ever again."

"No."

"Good enough." He took the bottle from the boy and got a look of disapproval from his wife. "Oh, I mean, you are grounded until you learn your lesson."

Life on a Chair

Life on a Chair

"How was the shower?"

"It was good."

"What type of good?"

"Is there only one type?"

"There is good that you were there and good because you can say you went."

"I am happy I went."

"They are quite a family. They are comical with how they act."

"Yeah, like the two sisters. You know Laurie…"

"We all know her."

"She asked me how I got there, so I told her I used the GPS, but of course, she doesn't use the GPS."

"Why would she? That would only mean that she gets to her destination on time."

"She still may be driving home now. Can you believe that she wanted me to follow her home?"

"That's crazy."

"I told her and her sister that I would, and then I went to the bathroom, and I just left after it."

"Good move."

"It was that, or telling them that I didn't want to follow them."

"A big girl like Laurie is not one you want to get upset."

"I know, right? Even though she is 70 now."

"I always forget how old she is."

"You forget a lot of things."

"Hey, I at least know when I am driving to use the GPS."

"Daniel had to show her how to get home. 'Go down about a half a mile, and make a left, but not a real left, only a half left, then you go straight for another mile, and then you are on the parkway."

"Not a real left; what does that even mean?"

"You know how a lane has three exits on it sometimes... He told her to stay and go on the left lane of the three."

"He knows the debate to have Laurie use technology is all but over."

"Oh, yeah. That ended before the GPS was even around. She came up to me and even said, 'Look at this. Look at this. I got the directions from Daniel for how to get here.' Apparently, he told her the directions on the phone call before they arrived."

"How was Christine?"

"Good. She is so nice. Right for Daniel."

"Yeah, I met her once or twice. Seems like a good fit for him."

"That family is something else, though."

"It is like a comedy show when you see them."

"It really is. Everything was fine here?"

"Yeah, I tried to get him to come out of his room, but you know him, he is not that type."

"He knows there is a world out there, right?"

"Maybe..."

"He is never leaving this place, you know that?"

"He had a weird look in his eyes when I saw him."

"Weird look?"

"You know, something was not right about him."

"Could be the lack of sunlight."

"Seriously though, I'm worried about him."

"Yeah, me too."

"He is too hard on himself."

"Yeah."

"He never enjoys life."

"Yeah."

"Everything is a business, a job to him."

"I know the problem."

"What?"

"He needs a girl. Someone to fool around with to take his mind off of things."

"Yeah. Maybe that would work. I just worry about him sometimes because my cousin had depression and killed himself at a young age."

"You think he has depression?"

"Maybe."

"You think he has something though?"

"Maybe."

"He is a young man with his whole life ahead of him; if he only knew how lucky he was."

"Yeah. He is too hard on himself."

"I'll talk to him in the morning."

"Okay."

In the basement, a young man stood on a chair, tying a knot.

"This better hold this time."

Before kicking the chair, he took one last look at the letter.

Farewell to this world, to this cruel cruel world, one where hard work is not rewarded, nepotism leads to success, and that awards nothing of goodness. Evil has taken over the world. Look around! Look around! Look around! The villains are the heroes, the heroes are mocked, and we are all led astray to the lake of fire.

I tried to fight the good fight. I tried to ward off the demons. But I cannot do that any longer. This world only ever gave me pain and misery. My cries for help were only met with whips of oppression and my cries were silenced by the ignorant. I am leaving this place, this cruel cruel place and for that, I am sure that none of you will note of my exit or care of my departure. What is to note of a departure such as mine?

My life has been a failure. I have been a failure. I let all my family and friends and all that ever knew me down. What once began with promise ends with this. It is only fitting that my death ends in nothing but silence and isolation. Where were the world's words when I needed them? Where were the crowds when I was alone?

Don't mourn my death nor cry of my life cut short, for you never celebrated my triumphs nor congratulated me on my success. I lived a life that was never known nor, seen, nor ever cared for by others. I leave you all, but I am not sure if I was ever really alive.

Trying to live a life for truth and, honesty and justice has led me to nothing but destruction, chaos and sadness, and with that, I leave you, you cruel, cruel world.

The rope held this time.

Night of an Aspiring Writer

Night of an Aspiring Writer

Why do you live? What is the reason that you wake up in the morning and put the energy of your strained body towards tasks that you may not even enjoy doing? Is it for the money that you obtain from your job? Could it be for the love that you have for your significant other? Is it for some reason that I am not sure of at the moment?

We all have to face this question at some point in our short lives where, all of a sudden, time flies by, and we are left with nothing but memories. I am not in any position of power to tell you why you should live and to what goals or functions you should devote your time. I have a few ideas, but at the end of the day, you must get up out of that bed yourself. You must face the world on your own. No amount of words from a writer can change that. It's your life, after all.

No matter how much you think that life is fruitless or the day is going to fail, you should always get up out of bed. Give life a chance, even when it doesn't give you one. You'll be surprised what great things can happen when you are open to them.

Before I get into a philosophical dialogue pertaining to the matter such as the one I mentioned, I would like to turn your attention to another, lighter topic. There is only so much philosophy one can take. My apologies to any reader who was interested in a potential dialogue.

F. Scott Fitzgerald, a writer that I am sure that the readers know, the renowned writer of one of the most popular books of all time that is taught in every school and sold in every store, had an unusual ending for a man so well-known today. You would think that he had a parade for when he died, like that of a soldier coming back from the war. He wrote of the Roaring '20s; the man should be held in high regard by many. With this idea of grandeur and celebration for the death of the famous writer, you would be wrong. He died in a very unceremonious way at the age of 44, a failure to no true acclaim to his name. The large gathering proves my point of such a desolate state. Only thirty people attended his lowly funeral like that of his iconic tragic hero, Jay Gatsby, who had no true friends, for the room was empty, and the saddest part of his life is that no one celebrated or mourned it when he died. He just left this Earth as if he were never here at all. A book not read, words not spoken, a life not lived. Thirty people attended the funeral of one of the most influential writers of our time. Can you believe that? You can probably name thirty people that you know right off the top of your head: your mother (who you only see on weekends), your father (who is always talking sports), your sister (who is busy working again), your brother (who is busy starting a baking company), your uncle (the one you saw at the park last week), your aunt (who you also saw at the park last week), your niece (whose name you don't know), your nephew (whose name you may remember), your cousin (who you never see), your grandma (who loves to make mashed potatoes), and your grandpa (who loves to sit in his favorite chair in the living room), and other members of family that I am sure you have; And of all of those people, all his mothers, fathers, brothers, uncles, aunts, nieces, nephews, cousins, grandmas, and grandpas only thirty showed up. Thirty to remember the man's time here. Thirty to walk down the aisle with his casket at their side. Thirty to put red and white flowers on his casket after the priest says a prayer. Thirty to be in the room for the wake that is held open to the public for two whole hours. Only thirty people came to show bountiful love, earned respect, observed hate, or anything for when the man died. His family or enemies did not think it was worth the time to show support for his departed soul or happiness for his untimely demise. He died, and the world reacted as if nothing happened.

I, for one, can think of no greater tragedy than that of ignorance of life. Many of us come across many different people. We love our friends and family who show that emotion back when they can. We have enemies who plot against us when we are not looking. They wish us failure, but they do acknowledge our presence here. To have no family or friends love you or enemies hate you is so sad. It begs the question, "Were you not good enough to be loved? Were you not bad enough to be hated? What the hell were you doing here all this time if you are neither loved nor hated?"

Now, Fitzgerald's book *The Great Gatsby* is a classic piece of American literature, a cornerstone of the American literary scene. All the schools have piles of books ready to be given to any student walking the hall, and children are instructed at an early age on the lessons while being shown its elegant prose. When people are asked about their favorite book by a surveyor polling the audience of a fellow comrade who wishes to seek the answer as part of good conversation, *The Great Gatsby* is bound to be mentioned, often with a reverence unusual for a book, like the reader knew they found a great book, like they know that the book contains the best literature can offer. Never do people mention a specific part of the book or any lines from it, but the book itself. The whole totality of the words composed between the bindings is enough to impress someone so that they remember it, but not enough to go into any details of the book, though. Imagine not knowing any lyrics to your favorite song but claiming rather it is the quality of the song that stands out more than any phrase or chorus. That is what people claim for the greatness of *The Great Gatsby.* Whenever I have addressed a person on this matter of why the book is so close to them, on why it is their favorite, they never elaborate, like how the theme of the American Dream is represented in the book, or how Gatsby is their favorite character, or how Caraway is a great narrator for the story, or even the description of the lavish parties, or the murder scene. Nothing, they only like the book. In fact, more people now answer it as their favorite book than when it was originally published. If you were to go back in time to the book's publication date and tell others of that era that *The Great Gatsby* is your favorite book, you would not get the subtle acceptance you do today. Stating the book as your favorite today is an expected situation when in a room full of readers. One of them loves the book. Having a room of thirty people of all ages, backgrounds, and households, and not one of them saying it is their favorite, is actually the rarity we have, instead of the unusual circumstance being something like having a book that is older than the reader being their favorite, or maybe just getting thirty people in a room who read on a regular basis. Some in the hypothetical past where you say that you love the book may even say that you would be the outsider in the scenario. Your standards as a reader may come into question since you like a book that at the time was not beloved by many. Similar to how you would get blank stares if you were to go back to Shakespeare's time and quote a sonnet. Today, we all know those words of love. *Shall I compare thee to a summer's day? Love is not love,* among others, because they have become a part of our society's fabric, how we come to identify ourselves, but that was not always the case. Our current interest in the book makes us believe its popularity was always on that level, that former generations knew and cared for it as much as we do, but they did not.

Let us now meet the character of this short work, the protagonist of this piece, who is tragic more for his mindset than his actions. He has been going by the name Jerry for most of his life. Aside from that one time in gym class in high school where he was called Jer by the teacher, a name he didn't much care for then but said nothing of as he sat on the sideline during the dodgeball game. If you see this man anywhere, whether at his job in a warehouse, or at his home, or when he is at the gym, the people call him Jerry, and if I am being completely frank, they say it in a very unconvincing, almost disappointing fashion. Like they know the man exists, they know who he is, they spoke to him a few times, and that is it.

Nothing more is ever wanted from Jerry. People respect Jerry. They like Jerry, but they don't respect or like him enough to be happy to see him.

Jerry has dreams, though, contrary to what most people would think. He wishes to be like that of F. Scott Fitzgerald and to write a great work of literature. He works hard on his craft and is diligent with it, focusing his attention on learning the classics and knowing all he can of the trends in the field, but I will say to you, the reader, that Jerry is most likely not going to make it as a writer. He doesn't know this yet, and his passion outweighs his lack of ability. As he is a young man, only in his early 20's this mistake is seen as a result of his ignorance, than any true talent. When no one reads him or cares for his words, whenever that day may be, our hero will learn the sad truth. He just isn't that good at writing.

We find the failed writer in a dark small room, lying in his bed with the blankets at his bare feet, with the lone light off, ready for sleep. His lean body, which can never seem to gain any weight, was prepared to shut down and call it a day for the current manual labor job he holds, which requires much strain on his body. Picking up boxes that weigh up to 50 pounds for multiple hours a day can cause pain for anyone's body; I don't care who you are. His fragile mind had other ideas instead of rest and wanted to stay awake to question his own life and meaning here, to present the fact that the end of Act 5 is closer than he thought, and Act 3, the climax of all he was, had already past him years ago. He may only be on hole 4 in age and feel like his putter is brand new and prepared for the greens, but he is already seeing the clubhouse.

As I said, his problem is mental as much as it is physical. He is not in Act 5. He is not even close to the clubhouse, but exhaustion makes him believe otherwise.

Why am I here? What am I doing? He asked as his head lay on his white pillow. *I am in over my head. I'm a failure. That's all there is to it: a failure, a loser.* He continued to himself. *I should end this right now. Just buy a gun and blow my brains out. This is not working, the job, the home, the life. I didn't sign up for this.*

When Jerry's mind gets this way, in such a state of depression and remorse, there is no way out; the darkness sinks into his mind and stays with him like a bad cold he can't get rid of. It hovers over his body like a cloud over a city, pouring negativity over each thought he has, not seeing any light in his life. He has had these disturbing thoughts before. Every couple of months, his anxiety from his lack of success in literature, exhaustion from working two jobs, and loneliness from having no friends combine so that all his rational thinking vanishes, like a man possessed, this damning hurt, this sudden strangeness encompasses his being. He does what he can to fight these demons by praying every night to the Christian God he had been brought up on. Demons do not like prayers praising God and Jesus. That is what his rational mind thought. He may be losing his mind, but he knows that the bad guys won't sway him if he is trying to talk to Jesus, to talk to his God, and to ask for help. His God may not help him out at the moment, but the demons will leave once he states he is not with them. His shattered soul, his hurt heart that is God's to have, not the demons. If they want it, they are going to have to go through the big fella. Despite his best efforts to learn the Lord's Prayer and the Hail Mary and repeating them to himself over and over again until the badness goes away, sometimes the demons get back up from the fight. Sometimes, the evil wins.

Also, I would like to mention that the reader can learn an insightful lesson from Jerry here. When you die, say the words, Jesus Christ. If you are in heaven, those around you will be glad to hear of the Messiah. If you are in Hell, they will run from the thought of him. If you are in purgatory, you will be alone and saying this to an empty room anyway.

Back to Jerry's situation, though.

What the hell am I doing with my life? Nobody will mind if I leave or if I decide to exit stage left. It is not like I do much here. I am really nobody important. Not like a politician or a celebrity. Just one bullet, right here. He motioned his hand to pretend to shoot his lower jaw through the back of his head. *Just one bullet could end all of this.*

His rational self started to fight the hurt insanity overpowering him. No. *No. No. I can't kill myself. Then I have to go to Hell. I hate that place, the Devil, the fire. Damnit. I don't want that.*

Jerry knew that his soul would not feel any better if he committed suicide and ended his physical body's time on Earth. He also never liked the lying, deceptive ways of the Devil or fire. He really hated fire. From what I hear from even heathens and heretics, not many would prefer Hell, either. On Earth, a man may be foolish enough to worship the Devil, to sell his soul, for fame and fortune, but that is only because the man wrongly believed that the pain in Hell is not as bad as it truly is. The scenes in movies, sounds of music, or words of novels can't express the horrors of that place, for they are thoughts expressed by a mortal man of an unworldly destination. Think of the most frightening, terrifying experience you can imagine. Hell is nothing compared to that because it has no limits for its evil; you, the describer of the scene, have limits. Don't underestimate the evil that is in Hell. It's there.

The Devil pisses me off with all his lying and deceiving. Bastard can go to Hell. He paused for a moment over his unexpected pun. Normally, it is an attack on a person's character, and if you say they can go to Hell, What is the expression if stated to the villain of the fiery inferno? Is it a compliment like saying a person's new furniture really fits the room? Perhaps it is a mistake, and you should have said that the Devil can go to heaven for the same effect, but even that seems out of place, for is heaven not where the Devil wanted to be all along? Or maybe it is only a pun, not to be read into more than I already have. I'd like to imagine the uncomfortable confrontation if the phrase was ever uttered with his company.

The Devil is standing before you, trying to convince you of his effective ways, why you should join him, and how Jesus wasn't all that great, and what do you spontaneously blurt out during his monologue?

"Look, join me. I am the ruler of Hell. You'll love it here. We have a warm environment, and the demons here are friendly when they aren't torturing people or being assholes. Do you really want to be an angel? I mean, do you want wings or some cool horns? Plus, what is better, to be an angel or kill one?" The Prince of Darkness says as he continues his long-winded pitch.

"Hell is the best place ever. I have been living here forever, since that whole episode with God, and look how I turned out." He would grin in a very unsettling way to hide the fact that his heart is cold and filled with hate. "We got great food here, and you'll get your own bed. All you need to do is give me your soul. I mean, let's be honest, it's not like you have been using it much anyway."

"Go to hell!" You tell the Devil, knowing that your heart is with the Lord. No pitch is worth the selling of your soul. Mother Mary and the Lord are who you love, not some guy on a throne with horns.

I can't help but wonder if you would laugh at the strange scene, though. As you are in Hell, you tell the Devil to go to Hell. He may not want someone that stupid at that point, so you may be in the clear. But I digress.

For a brief moment, Jerry's depression was gone. His regular wit of self-deprecation and short-spoken wisdom was back, and he was the same good, humble, respectful man many have come to like, but just as quickly as it came, it left, and he envisioned a world without him and how little he meant to it all.

So what then? If I can't kill myself? I'm stuck here. In this shithole of a world, with all the bullshit with the lies from the beginning to the end? Where disagreements happen over everything, from what book to get at the library to what country to invade? Hate is common here because man is common here. What am I going to miss? All the robbers, rapists, and run-of-the-mill criminals? If I kill myself, I go to

Hell, but if I stay, I, well, am still here. Oh goddamnit! My luck is that Hell rejects me because I only killed myself. They'd probably rather have murderers, molesters, and monsters instead of me. I really hate fire.

He got up from his bed and turned on the light, hoping that some visible cues could help him steer his sinking ship in the right direction. All he needed was actual light to open his eyes to his wrongful opinion of himself.

The desperate writer sat down on the desk chair, doing what he could to be positive but also knowing that the only thing stopping his attempt was a pistol and a bullet.

He took out a prayer card of the Mother Mary from the desk drawer, and held it in his hand for a moment. He always felt a deeper connection to her, for some reason, than any other part of the faith. A connection even deeper to that than Jesus. When he thought of her, a light would always seem to be lighter. His hope restored. His life renewed. He hoped that she would help him again.

After saying her prayer, he hummed the melody of the lyrics to a Beatles song; when *I find myself in times of trouble, Mother Mary comes to me, speaking words of wisdom, let it be.* Jerry knows that this line is not speaking of the Virgin Mary but of the singer's mom; still, he can't help but make it about the mother of our creator, especially when the Devil is getting the better of him. He closed his eyes and took a deep breath, trying to fight the darkness around him.

Jerry then opened his eyes and glanced at his bookshelf of classic literature, of Shakespeare's plays, Twain's Finn adventures, and Hemingway's short stories, until he got to *The Great Gatsby*, his favorite book. He always felt an odd connection to the main character, how he had it all: the money, the fame, the parties, yet he had nothing at all. The whole world seems to care about him, yet no one does. He tries to do right, yet never gets anywhere, only farther away from the love he dreams of daily. The only progress he ever takes is one that gets him closer to a mechanic wrongly accusing him of cheating and then killing him as if the world is against him. No matter what he does, he will lose. The endless money, the boundless fame, the non-stop parties can't change that. He is bound to only one death, one of an empty room of his lost soul without an obituary in the newspaper or a tear from a friend.

I can't explain why the hero has this connection to the character, and I don't know if he can either. Like that of the Virgin Mary, it is something that he just feels. Whether you wish to take that as actual proof or the rambling of a madman is up to you.

He stared at the side cover of the novel in its dark blue bold letters facing vertically in the middle of the white backing, and the author's name in the same blue color with a more common, no bold, slimmer font at the top and the publishing house's trademark, a capital letter S at the bottom, and for a second his depression, and thoughts that gave him only doubt, worry and fear, were gone. He recalled the inspiration that the book gave him as a young, naïve writer, how he idolized Fitzgerald for such a literary accomplishment and still does.

Fitzgerald would want me to read him. He thought. *Yeah. I can't do that to him.* He looked at all the books of all the classic writers he had collected over the years, including Shakespeare, Twain, Hemingway, and Fitzgerald. *Someone has to read all those classics. It is an insult to all these greats if no one does.*

He nodded to himself as if to affirm that he had come to his senses. He put the prayer card back in the drawer and climbed back into bed, shut his brown eyes, and fell asleep for the night, avoiding what would have been the biggest mistake of his life: letting his sadness destroy his hope and not seeing that all those in life have hard times, from those wordsmiths on the bookshelves of many readers, young and old, to those aspiring wordsmiths, with their notepads and incomplete manuscripts, dreaming of literary greatness, to those who know not of a wordsmith's struggle, who are impressed by the notion of a friend being published and who strive for excellence in their field, day in and day out. They all have bad days where nothing goes right, tough times they struggle to get through, and dark moments they feel more like demons than angels, and where they relate a lot more to Cain than to Abel. Scenes where the edge of the cliff is only there to fall from. Where God has seemingly abandoned them, and their life seems pointless. That hurt, that persistent pain, that confusion of one's own place in this world, is a part of life. You have only truly lived when you learn to overcome it. When you cure the wounds, overcome the bad, and look the Devil in the eyes and say, "Not today. Close, but not today." For no one should ever give up on themselves, no matter how much it seems the world has given up on them.

Jerry may never be the writer that Fitzgerald was. He may never become much of a writer at all. He will most likely give up on the trade and decide that a life of consistency is more for him. And there is nothing wrong with that, for the world can't be full of only writers. Who will make roads that the writers travel on? Who will deliver the mail that the writer reads? Who will repair the house that the writer lives in? Writers write of our world, but they are far from the only ones that make it. No matter what anyone does in this world, from the construction worker paving another street to the mailman delivering another envelope to the handyman installing another attic, they cannot give up on their lives or on themselves, for thirty people may not seem like a lot, but thirty people are still thirty people. That is thirty people who thought that, yes, your life here was worth it and that they felt you were a part of it. You impact others more than you know.

Back when Fitzgerald wrote *The Great Gatsby*, when he wrote to his friend how he doesn't think the book is rotten, when he couldn't think of a proper name for it, I'm not sure if suicidal prevention was his purpose, if he ever imagined he would be the last thing that a person would use to find meaning in their life, but on this night, his words helped a man who needed them the most. They saved a man for they inspired him to continue to live.

Plus, I'm sure that Mother Mary played a part in it, too.

Blue Curtain 

Blue Curtain

A teacher stood at the front of the classroom, reading the words of the classic writer to a room of disinterested students. Of the thirty kids, only about five were listening to the 30-something-year-old overemphasize the works of the dead writer. The acting reject was at the point in the classic story where the hero found himself awake in a new room, and the author was merely describing the scene to the reader. Now, there is a caveat to this rather ordinary reading in that the writer had an unstable personality during their life, and scholars could interpret him better by understanding his use of words. They found that the writer would often describe certain scenes of sadness and depression differently from talking about happiness and joy. Coincidently, the production of these scenes always revolved around a part of the author's life that had an event of a similar nature. When the writer was sad personally, he wrote of sad things in his story, although not obvious to the average reader. When the writer was happy in his personal life, he wrote of joy and goodness. There are theories as to whether the author's own mind knew of this occurrence or not.

The teacher was taught this part of the writer's life when she learned of him in college. She knew this well. In fact, that was one of the aspects of the story that she enjoyed telling others. His stories are not only an examination of his societal critiques or storytelling but of his own journey through life. She has even heard of a group of scholars trying to establish a curriculum around the events of the author's life with his books. He wrote a book shortly after his son died. He wrote one while he was getting married. Among others, that all could be explained through the lens of a man struggling with his own life as much as telling a story. The teacher believed that this unique way of approaching a classic writer would intrigue some kids. She was wrong. Kids only view classic authors as dead people they are forced to read for homework. The mind of a kid is too naïve and young to understand the words of an adult, no matter whether they are a genius or not. The kid's understanding of the world is limited, so no matter how much the writer tries, at the end of the day, they are only dealing with a kid, one that when they hear of a bad word, you must remind them not to say it, or one that has a hard time sitting still in a chair, or that find tests they take during the day to be the worst things in their lives.

"You see when he wrote about blue curtains, that means that he was sad." She explained the scene. "We know this because this author always expressed his emotions in subtle ways. Do you all remember that other story we read of him about the guy at the hotel pool?" No one acknowledged her question. "That had a sunny day, and sunny days to this author meant happiness. He often described his own sadness with items such as dark clothing, like blue or black. So we know that this story was written during a time in the author's life when he was dealing with a personal loss or a hard time."

A student in the back of the room, who had only listened to half of what was said, called out, "What if the author wrote that the curtains were blue because they were actually blue? I mean, why do we have to think that the guy was really interested in the color of the curtains?"

The teacher always hears this question and is tired of answering it. She can't stand that the one kid who always asks this question never asks anything else during the school year. When there is time for review, she hears nothing from this kid, but now, when this author is brought up with this particular scene of blue curtains, there is always that one kid who feels they came across something unique in their question. Why does this author's use of a certain cloth intrigue a certain kid every time she teaches the book? Perhaps that is a topic for the group she heard of.

Can it really be that the author who wrote of sadness and happiness, who wrote of love and life and all in between, and had his life in his stories came upon an unusual curiosity of the human mind as he wrote this scene of the blue curtains? Could it be that people are just fascinated so much with curtains that whenever they are brought up in stories, everything stops, and they all notice the curtains? Can we be wrong with our evaluation of ourselves, of what we are, and where we are going? We do not care about questions of God and his nature or of the universe and its vastness. Get rid of the poets and their words of love and hope, and turn off all the music that makes us dance and feel depressed. No, that is not what is on our minds; curtains, we are thinking about the colors of curtains this whole time.

Back in the classroom, a most unusual event occurred when a hole, something you would see in a sci-fi movie that has access to other dimensions, and I am quite sure the writing community is making up, opened up, and outwalked the author to the blue curtain story.

The man was a little bit older than he was in the picture at the back of the book, where he had slick back hair. But now, the man had some gray in his hair and was a little stockier than you would have imagined, as none of the photos showed him above the waist. Whether this man was fat or husky is something that may need some discussion in that group the teacher wants to start. Despite his older age and extra pounds, he still had the mean smile of a guy who was not to be messed with. The guy has taken a life and thought nothing of it and has punched and been punched before.

Those who have physical prowess where they have encountered the pain of others always have a subtle confidence in their smile, a minor confidence in their walk, that if you don't look carefully, you may miss. Some who only have this in their life to their name and are not of the mental capacity to think are so proud to flaunt this characteristic that even the pacifists notice it. The author of the blue curtain story had enough sanity in him to know how to hide his insanity and how to mask his arrogance, knowing that if push came to shove, he could kick your ass. And if that didn't work, he would pull a gun on you, which certainly would end the confrontation.

The teacher failed to tell the kids the part of the man's life where his vicious behavior showed. The author had hunted and killed for part of his life. There are stories he wrote about how he took the lives of animals and was quite proud of the act. If you are lucky, you can buy a rare picture of him with an animal hunted at one of those rare bookstores that carries that kind of stuff. From what I know, the man killed numerous elephants, many deer, and antelopes, once fought a crocodile, and had the coats of a few larger cats, like a lion and tiger. The last part of the coat is debated today, as no one knows if the author killed the animals themselves or was a part of the group that committed the act, and the author never elaborated clearly on this when asked about it in interviews. There is even a claim that the author even killed a man once earlier in his life before he was known as a writer, and in a time when you could kill someone in an empty part of town late at night and then leave the town, and then nobody knows it was you. He got into an altercation with the guy, blows were exchanged, and the opposing guy didn't get back up from his fall. Like the lion and tiger coat, this story is to be met with skepticism, for the man who was proclaimed dead in the town that the author was in was not dead when the author left the bar, but rather reports show the other fighter died of a heart attack, a few days later. On the other hand, the town in question celebrates the occasion by naming the bar after the author. According to the townspeople, the author took down a man who was about to commit a crime in the establishment, so the murder was self-defense and justified. Plus, the author became a household name years later in his life, so the bar could use the recognition. I hear that the bar goes as far as to say that the author even included it in several of his bestselling books. If you were to ask the author of this event in his lifetime, he would vehemently deny that he killed a man, only that he defended himself that night. The author was tough, but how much his toughness was to a legend, as compared to real events, is something up for a reader to decide.

The author had heard of the student's comments on his work. And he didn't appreciate it.

"Excuse me, child. But who are you to question this woman, this scholar of my words? By questioning her, you question me, and I will not allow it."

No one in the classroom moved since the dead author walked over to the ignorant student and notably was not dead. He was not a zombie coming back to life or an actor playing a hoax on anyone. This was not a hologram of the author by the teacher to fool the class. This was him, in all his flesh and blood, as though he was not dead and buried six feet under but as alive as everyone else in the classroom.

The kids were scared because a man that is supposed to be dead is now in their classroom. Although there were some kids who didn't recognize him, as they didn't even pay attention to the story he wrote, they were aware enough to know that the stranger in the room was pissed and directed his anger toward them. Add that to the fact there is some sort of portal to another dimension in the room. Yeah, it is a lot for a kid to take in who normally raises his hand once the entire year and barely even studies for the class. I get why the students said nothing.

"Who are you? I say, who are you, child?" The author commanded the frightened kid, nearly yelling.

"Jonathan Smith."

"Exactly! You are nobody! A fly on the wall, an ant on the ground! You are nothing today; you were nothing when you were born, and you shall remain nothing when you die! How dare you question my timeless work and act as if I was going through this half-ass! This book is older than you and will outlive you, you stupid child! You ignorant, insolent!" The author pointed at the teacher, who was speechless. "Listen to what his woman has to say! You may learn a thing or two."

The author walked back over to the hole as he looked at the teacher who was hiding behind her desk. "I must teach this kid a lesson."

He then pulled out a shotgun and, with two shots, emptied out the gun, and the annoying child was no more.

"To solve a problem is to find a solution, and the best way to find a solution is to rid the problem of being. If you remove the problem, there is no problem." The author explained to the classroom, who were all hiding from him. He threw the shotgun over his shoulder as though he finished his hunt for the day.

A voice came from the hole, "And we will now continue with the divorce settlements."

The author, with the shotgun still in hand, shrieked as though he was the one afraid. "Goddamnit!" And he ran into the hole, which closed behind him.

Many taught of parts of the writer's life, from when he was hopeful in his youth and worked alongside those in reporting, to happy at his wedding when he celebrated the success of his first classic novel as well, to sad in his drunken years where alcohol take up all his words and time, for he wrote great novels from each era of his life during those times. None ever spoke of the dark stories that consisted of violence and gore and were very unlike anything else that the classic author wrote. They were not acceptable to teach in a school, for they were not for children or anyone for that matter. The author wrote these when he was going through his divorce.

In a quiet room sat a man at his desk that had nothing on it but his typewriter. He leaned on his chair as he grabbed his flask, reviewing his words. He was done for the night and would finish his story another time.

"What if one day, someone who doesn't understand me will read these words and not give me my proper credit? You know there is going to be some wiseass who thinks I didn't put any effort into any of this. That is people for you." He took a drink from his flask. "I will simply have to go to that time period in the future and teach them a lesson, that is all." He laughed at the thought. "Yeah, like that could ever happen."

Mask Burning

Mask Burning

The ending of a situation has come to be a fascination that humanity cannot stop thinking about. Whether we are contemplating the end to our own lives, the very society we are in, or to a story we are being told, we simply can't get over asking, "How does it end?"

Now, we don't know about the ends of our own lives. There could be a heaven, one in which the Lord and angels dwell, waiting for the end of days, but it's not like I have been there for vacation, so that is only a guess, really. We could end our modern lives of luxury and ease that allows for cars and cell phones to be as much of our identity as that of water and food with nuclear war (one that the skies light up like the Fourth of July, only instead of their being a song to sing about freedom afterward, there is no one around) Or maybe some natural disaster will lead to the lack of resources we need to survive and the very system we know collapses unto itself, and we are not living in a golden age as many of us view, but a house of cards, that with just the right push can lead to famine and crop failure and livestock dying. If there is a third world war of large government powers with weapons too powerful for man, there is not going to be a fourth one soon after it since there will most likely not be any of us after the third world war. We do know how this story ends, though. The kids burn their masks to represent the end to COVID.

Is it really the end of COVID? What about the variant still going around?

There are still some who are wearing masks, though. What about them?

You know what, why don't you just read the damn story? I am not a doctor with my white robes and charts and office with tips on how to live a healthier life. I won't tell you that you have diabetes or, that you should cut back on sugar, or that the medication you are taking is not working. That is not me. I am the narrator, the recipient of the news to which I am telling. I can only tell you the character's story as it unfolds; I can't cure diseases or help you with any of that sort of stuff. If you have questions about medical stuff, you should probably consult a doctor (although with how some handled COVID, that may not be the most sound advice I ever gave)

I don't know if this is the end of COVID, really. I am not going to talk to you about the variant here. I can't explain why some people still wear masks despite not having to.

I can tell you that on one late June afternoon, a party took place for a kid that was supposed to commemorate the end of COVID. Freddy was turning 11, and his mom thought that there would be no better way to celebrate his birthday than to have a bunch of kids over the house and burn their face masks. The face masks have become a symbol of the virus that destroyed the year 2020. By eliminating them, the people at the party are symbolically killing COVID. I mean, sure, if that is what the partygoers are into, then who am I to judge? I am the asshole who questions drinking games that revolve around the act of throwing a ball into a red cup across the table because I like to get drunk without cups or balls being thrown, so what do I know? Of course, Freddy's mom would be responsible for burning the masks, as the kids would not be allowed too close to the fire, but nevertheless, the masks would be burning at 11-year-old Freddy's party.

Freddy's parents, Jennifer and George, agreed that the party would be best for the children, which is, of course, another way of saying that Jennifer liked the idea, and George went with it.

There is one person who is not too keen on the idea of this party, Freddy's uncle, Kel. He didn't agree with the whole charade, not because of the possible dangers of the virus or the dangers of the kids spreading it. No, he was upset because the event had to happen at his house, for no other reason than he is one of the two brothers who have a large backyard where the burning of masks would be no problem. Yeah, Uncle Kel didn't care about the COVID virus. He was more upset that kids were coming over to his house. The guy barely talks to his neighbors (aside from Tommy), and now his house is going to be filled with parents of people he doesn't know. At least Kel will have alcohol available to him.

Of all of the kids, it was Freddy that Uncle Kel liked. He could tolerate the naïve youngster as the two sat at the kitchen table eating breakfast as their mother prepared the fire outside. Neither wanted to help her since they knew once they did, they would be helping her the rest of the day. They both ignored her, knowing that the responsibility for the party setup would fall on George if they said nothing.

"So, how was the school year? Aside from the fact that the pandemic killed any chance of you enjoying it." Uncle Kel asked his nephew.

"It was ok."

"Learn anything interesting?" He asked, not really interested.

"I learned that when you say less after a word, it means that there is none of it."

"Oh.... You spend a whole year of schooling for something like that. Your mom must be proud."

The kid ignored the adult at the table. "Pointless means that the thing has no point. Fruitless means no fruit."

"Mindless means no mind."

"Oh, yeah. But that wasn't an example the teacher gave us." Freddy continued to eat his cereal.

"They wouldn't want to spell it out for all of you, I guess."

They both sat there for a bit until the uncle tried to change the topic of the conversation.

"What else has been going on in your life?"

"I got a new video game."

"Really?"

"Yeah. The hero has to explore the seven worlds of Akira. Each world has a crystal, and by gathering the seven crystals, you can defeat the main boss. Each world has its own boss, though, so each time you get a crystal, the next boss is harder to beat."

"Of course." The uncle was lost on his nephew's description of a game until then; he didn't know existed.

"You have to collect different outfits and weapons since each world is made of a different element."

"Why wouldn't it be?"

"My friend Harry says that if you beat the game on normal and then play it on hard, there is another extra main boss. Isn't that cool?"

"Look, I don't mean to burst your bubble, but you're a kid, and I don't care about what you care about."

"Oh."

"Kid, the stuff you think about is so stupid and pointless that it is practically equal to not thinking. Now, you may think I am being an asshole, but when you're older, you'll understand." He sipped his cup of coffee. "Kids are stupid pieces of shit that are only good so that we can continue to have more of us here. The only reason they even have schools is that kids are too useless to have real responsibility at your age. We can't put you on farms, and the days of having you work in the factories are over. We have no other place for you kids than school. Unfortunately, you don't learn that until you are done with it."

"So, what is something I should learn?"

Kel muttered to himself, "The teacher obviously missed the word useless, too."

The mom, Jennifer, entered from the outdoors. "Are either of you going to help me? Kel, can you get up off your butt and help a little?"

"Oh, I was actually going to show Freddy here the gift I got him."

"You were?" Freddy asked, surprised.

The two rushed into the other room, avoiding the kid's mother.

"So, what did you get me?" Freddy asked about his gift.

"What?"

"What did you get me?"

"Oh, nothing. It's a surprise."

"So you said this to get out of helping my mom?"

"Pretty much." They both sat down on the couch. "I'll be honest with you; I don't even want to have the party here; setting it up is another thing altogether."

"What, you don't like my friends?"

"Kid, I barely like you. Kids are nothing more than reminders that you either had sex with someone you didn't like or that the genes you thought were great are pretty bad. Plus, you have no idea how much you kids cost."

"I am starting to see why you never had kids," Freddy commented.

"Hey, I got something to show you. Something you may like." Uncle Kel got up from the table and headed to the counter. He picked up a baseball card that was sealed shut. "Look at this baseball card I just bought. Do you know who this is?"

"No." The kid said, disinterested.

"Oh, come. I thought you liked baseball."

"Nah. Not really."

"Then you are going to be disappointed in what I got you for your birthday."

The two then sat on the couch, unsure of what to say to one another. The uncle wanted to talk about the new baseball card that he spent a lot on, while his nephew wanted to talk about his new video game.

"Well, this card is the most valuable card around. And I just bought it." Kel bragged to the kid, who didn't understand anything about the card.

"Why would you buy a baseball card? That is silly."

"This card is priceless." He handed the card to the kid to inspect.

"So it has no price?"

"In a way, yes. See, a thing that people do is to get as many priceless things as possible, and those with the most priceless things are considered the most important people."

"But if the things have no price, how can you tell the difference between something with a price and something without it?"

"My nephew, you have learned a valuable lesson today. Stuff doesn't matter. We only think it matters, which then makes it matter."

"Even though it doesn't really matter."

"Exactly."

"Wait, so what actually matters?"

He took back the baseball card. "Freddy, my friend, if you figure that one out, let me and everyone else on this earth know."

The mom came in from outside, "Your dad better be back from the store soon since neither of you is helping me."

"How about we catch an early movie?" The uncle suggested to the birthday boy.

George came in with two full bags of party gear. "Boy, have I got a bunch of stuff for this party?"

"Unless you want to stay here?" The uncle repeated.

Freddy noticed all the stuff that his dad was putting on the table. "What's playing?"

The uncle and nephew headed for the door as the uncle shouted to the dad across the room. "I am taking the kid to see a movie. Bye."

The two went to see a movie that neither really liked, but that was better than spending all day setting up the decorations for the party. The unfortunate other two, the mom and dad, were stuck handling the party affairs. Both were exhausted when the first guests came over.

The party has started. A mid-afternoon barbeque dinner of hot dogs and burgers was already being served. All the kids were over by the food, getting what they could eat. In part of the large backyard, three men stood staring at the fire, plates in their hands. There was George, the father of the birthday boy, Uncle Kel, and the neighbor, Tommy, who had no kids but knew of the party and was friends with Kel.

Tommy asked the question everyone had. "So your wife thought it was a good idea to have the kids burn their masks at this party?"

"She is calling it a "mask burning" It is to bring in a new era of our happiness and end COVID."

"Oh... sure."

"That is so stupid." Uncle Kel responded right away.

"Of course it is! But I want to be able to sleep in my own bed tonight."

"Fair enough." Tommy understood. "Being with a woman is the toughest thing for any man to handle."

"Right, like you know anything about that. The most you are with a woman is when you get those massages by those Asian women in the shopping center."

"How are those by the way?" George asked, knowing the answer.

"Not bad. They keep getting more expensive."

"No Tommy, you are getting cheaper and freakier. When are you going to settle down already?"

"Not now. I don't want to hear it."

Tommy has been a notorious bachelor most of his life, even before meeting Kel, who, although he had his faults, was happily married up until five years ago.

"Come on, Tommy, you can't call getting a happy ending from an Asian girl a real relationship."

"As compared to putting up this party where masks are burned for some symbolic meaning. Are you guys sure we are not going to offer one of those kids up to God?"

Kel has been trying to get the man to settle down and not only go where his second brain wants for that day, but Tommy has been reluctant to accept his friend's offer. Tommy doesn't push back on Kel, and neither does George, on the obvious issue of him moving on.

"Did I tell you guys that I got a mint condition rookie card of Ken Griffey Jr?"

"Wow, that must be worth a lot."

"Oh, and by the way, your kid doesn't like baseball."

"I know that," George answered.

"Well, I didn't."

The guys looked at the rare baseball card.

"How did you get this?" Tommy asked.

"I bought it from a dealer online."

Jennifer then called all the kids together to get their masks. There was some resentment from some of the boys who felt that they could put their masks in the fire all by themselves, but Jennifer knew better than to allow that to happen. All the parents stood as she put masks in the fire, which was admittedly less than spectacular. The scene went on for another few minutes as Jennifer tried not to put all the masks in the fire at once. The only parent not in the backyard for the burning was Uncle Kel, who had one too many beers and was lying down inside.

A girl from a parent that Uncle Kel didn't know or care to know came running inside. When she saw the middle-aged man on the couch, she called out to him. "Hey, did you see that fire! It was because of all the masks!"

"No. Really? I had no idea. This whole time, I thought our neighbor's house was burning."

Freddy came into the room as excited as the girl. "Did you see those flames? They were so high."

"What did you kids never see a freaking fire before?" Uncle Kel complained.

"What are you putting in the fire?" Freddy asked the girl.

"I don't know. I'm looking for something." She left the room, continuing her search.

Freddy directed his attention to his uncle. "Mom said that we could put one extra item in the fire if we wanted."

"Sounds exciting." The uncle said, disinterested in his nephew's fire or new girlfriend. "Son of a bitch has the kids doing a peace offering."

"So I put in that priceless baseball card you showed me earlier."

"You what?" He leaped up from the chair.

"Yeah, I figured you wouldn't mind because you said it had no price."

The uncle covered his face with his hands. "Because priceless..."

His nephew finished the thought, "Means it has no price."

"Of course it does." Kel smacked his hand against his forehead.

The girl came back into the room with a whiffle ball bat. "Mind if I burn this?"

"No problem. I don't even like baseball."

The Painting of Peace and Destruction

The Painting of Peace and Destruction

A renowned artist, a man of many disciplines of the craft, looked outside of his studio at the world that is nothing more than a battlefield for the decrepit and the future lost. The plazas that were once filled with poets speaking rhymes and artists drawing of the town's life are gone, filled with men in boots carrying guns. No more are families in the city roaming around delighting in the shops with their deals and various items on sale, enjoying their days in each other's company as much as anything that the stores can give them. Peace was no more here. It left. It went with the last of the citizens. Now, all that roam are soldiers ready to take whatever they can from whoever gets in their way. These machine men are not even of this nation either, but of a foreign one that has been bent on world domination for the past few years. And the scary thing is, they may be close. They have strangled the world, hoping to cause it to suffocate, and Mother Earth may just pass out.

Alone in an art studio, we find the middle-aged artist sitting in the chair in the corner. He knew that his home would be ransacked soon. It was only a matter of time. He had missed the last way out of here a month or two ago when the invaders started to take over. Before then, the townspeople told him of the coming destruction, but he did not leave. There are others in some homes and apartments that are found by the invaders, and they are treated with cruelty as though they were pigs to the slaughter, not people of the world.

He spoke to his paintings, the only living things left in the town besides himself. "When they come, they will destroy all of my work, all of my art. All of my life. I gave this craft my heart and soul, for not a day went by when I did not sketch paint, or create beauty of this world. But alas, that beauty shall die with me and my friends who remain with me." He slowly walked around, examining his paintings. "What monsters of war see the enemies as less than themselves? Are we not all from Adam? Are we all, not the Lord's people? And yet I am not even human to these people." He looked at his hands. "My hands don't bleed as a person, nor does my face wrinkle as one. I don't feel or love with my soul, according to those who will destroy me and my life's work. It is as if I am nothing more than cattle to these people. For when they come knocking down that door, I will be left to surrender, and all of this, all of you." He looked around at his small art studio, with its sketches, paper, and brushes. "They will destroy all that I make, all that you are. They can destroy me and the art that I have, but can they destroy what some wish this world to be?" Bombs went off outside of the room.

"I draw for peace, to explore the world through colors and lines, but they fight for destruction, to see this nation and every other nation bow to them. Art shall always live on." He put his hand on one particular painting." You shall live on, friend. No pen is needed for the poet to write. No paper is needed for the artist to draw. No piano is needed for a musician to play. For the art is inside." He said to the empty room and filled canvas. "Men try to conquer the world, but no man can ever conquer art. It belongs to all men. We belong to all men."

He heard footsteps outside of his door. They were here. He knew this was it. His life and art would die here.

"Every room! Every room is to be searched!" He heard a voice holler.

He sat waiting for his enemies, those of the world without art, and knew they would knock down the door at any minute. Would he run? Would he hide like he heard some do? No, for when you see evil, you do not hide from it but confront it and say that you are not afraid of the evil or darkness before you. No matter how much that the fear is there, you cannot allow the fear of evil to creep into your heart. Evil may kill you, but it can never take your soul.

That is why the painter sat in his chair in the corner of his empty yet full room. He wanted his enemies to know that he was not afraid of them and their ability for catastrophe. He can't defend himself. He has no guns, but he also has no fear of them. You can never really kill a man if you never have his soul.

"Every room!" He heard called out.

His end will come, and for a moment, he wondered what would become of his body when they killed him. Surely, these monsters would not give him a chance to live, and they may burn his works. Will they even give his art life to live in them? For a moment, he worried that perhaps he was wrong in all of this.

What if they do win in this war and all that the opponents do is fruitless to stop them? What if the bad guys, those that harbor hate from the rest of the world, actually come out on top here? I am assuming that somehow, the side that shared my views will come out on top. What if that doesn't happen? There is a distinct possibility that I have picked the losing side in this conflict. What if these monsters actually win? That can't happen, can it?

Then the shouting stopped, and the artist remained sitting, hearing nothing but the pounding of his heart. Sure, he can try not to be afraid; in his mind, he is as tough as ever and ready for all they throw at him, but his heart, the core of his physical body, was pounding faster than ever, for he knew these were his last breaths and last moments of life.

They would intrude on his studio at any minute. All he could hope for was that they would shoot him right away, for he would never allow them to take him prisoner. He heard rumors that this enemy is so cruel to their captives that many are afraid of them not for their firepower but for the torture they will give any who oppose them. Their fear is as powerful as any weapon they hold.

Yet no slamming came at his door. No one burst into his room. He remained alone in his full art studio.

Had they not found him? Did they somehow miss his studio? Was he really going to be free in this warzone he found himself in? Was there some confusion in the lines? Is his studio somehow being blocked from the enemy's vantage point? Is there a force he doesn't know that is fighting the enemy? What was actually going on since they should have knocked down his door by now?

For a brief moment, the artist sat confused about what was happening, for if these enemies were as thorough as rumored, they would have found him out and quite possibly killed him on the spot. He knows of a few that have met a horrific fate.

Then a Nazi soldier, no older than a recruit, with no dirt on his uniform and a helmet too small for his head, slowly opened the door to the room of the painter, who remained silent as the man approached.

The soldier spoke up, in a high-pitched nervous tone, "Hello, civilian." He cleared his throat to sound more formal. "Hello, civilian. We, the soldiers of the Fuhrer, are doing checks on any of the buildings on this block. This is a war zone now, soon to be the property of the Third Reich, the Fuhrer, and all that is Germany." He didn't look directly at the artist, whose nerves resided a little when he saw the age of the kid. This was not a soldier he dealt with, not a seasoned veteran, not a man of culture, but a boy with as much experience goofing around with his friends and drinking as he does holding a gun and standing in formation. The youth continued to be more nervous than the artist whose property he had broken into. "You, civilian, are at the risk of being under attack by the barrage of gunpowder and other weapons that are to be made in this area soon."

The artist said nothing of the irony he had witnessed. His creative life was under attack when this Germanic nation rose and used fear to force capture most of Europe. He can't risk being under attack when he is already under attack.

Neither spoke to the other. And after a few moments of standing completely still, the naïve soldier broke form and walked around the room of paintbrushes and sketches when he stopped at the largest painting in the room, intrigued by its large size that filled the entire wall and the black and white coloring that gave it a dire, yet realistic tone.

"Who made this?" The young soldier asked the man.

"You did." The artist said sternly to the soldier, still not looking right at him.

"No way." The naïve infantryman walked up closer to the painting. "I feel like I would remember painting this." The newly formed soldier of the Blitzkrieg stared at the painting, trying to recall a time when he would have painted the masterpiece. When in all his training did he ever learn to paint? "This is pretty good, eh?" He motioned at the artist who sat there, angry for the intrusion of evil into his home and for the man's lack of awareness of his art. "I actually remember making this." The soldier pointed at the painting as he spoke. "See, these eyes are looking at these eyes, and then there are these eyes that are staring at you. The whole thing is about eyes looking at each other from different angles. That is why I made this, to talk about eyes. Cause when you think about it, what are you without your eyes? Nothing really."

The artist said nothing as he hid the true meaning behind his painting.

The soldier's superior, a man of much older age, entered the room. You could tell that this man was older in his composure and his general way about him, for the gunshots and destructive scenes didn't phase him. He knew of the strategy and horrors of war. He knew of the grimness of death. The war had become a part of him. He had killed many men in this conflict, the first being his former self, who once knew of art and culture instead of ammunition and machine guns. "What are you doing? We are expected back to base."

"Hey, look at this. I made this painting." The younger soldier stood right in front of it.

The older soldier had gone to school for art before the Nazi regime took over his life, and he knew of the significance of the artist and the art and, most importantly, that his bonehead comrade didn't have anything to do with its production. "That's a Picasso, you jackass."

"But this guy said I made it."

"It is an anti-war masterpiece. You and me are soldiers fighting a war. That is what he meant."

The artist stayed silent, bitter that the two had not left his house yet, but also worried that they would take him captive after their back and forth.

"Oh…. Right… I knew that." The uninformed soldier headed for the door. "Hey, but doesn't that mean that this guy is Picasso? Doesn't the Fuhrer want him dead?"

The superior soldier knew of the man's identity, and before evil took over his country, he respected the artist. Before the famine and the war, it was Picasso who he wanted to be, and he went to art classes in Germany during his youth. He enjoyed walking through the plazas of the city and see the magnificent colors of the painting.

But not anymore, for his life is now with the army. Never does he utter his past fascination with art to any of his fellow soldiers, for that will get him in trouble. He was on assignment to pick up all his soldiers, do a check on the area, and head to the base. The location of Picasso was still unknown to the leaders.

I can't tell you how he kept that artistic part in him, if he even kept it at all, after all the training, all the war, and all the death. How does anyone keep sane when they live among insanity? How can you keep a part of your identity that you know not of? If enough time goes by, do you not lose that essential part of you since you never use it? I thought that you forget words in a foreign language if you don't repeat them on a consistent basis. I could be wrong here. Regardless, this soldier kept his fire for creativity in him, even though he lived in a dark, gloomy world where originality was seen as taboo. He kept it enough to still be able to identify the artist, at least.

For a second, the soldier did not speak as a soldier but as a student. "No. This man is not Picasso."

"But you said…."

"Are you arguing with me, major?" He went back into line with the same menacing voice that got him his current position.

"No, sir." The foolish young soldier answered.

"Good. Now, head out."

The two men of different worlds were left in the room together. One room, two men, and two different ways of their life. Picasso, in his plain bare clothes, had nothing more than his paintbrush and mind to speak of the actions around him. The Nazi soldier, with his stylish uniform, and a man that has become a cog in a machine bent on world domination, no matter how brutal or harsh it may be. One man represented creativity and hope for what art could be. The other was a harsh reality of where the efforts have gone in this world: to firepower and young men's boots. One expresses himself through the peaceful stroke of a brush. The other follows an order by the march of their feet and the reloading of their gun.

"Mister, I advise you or anyone you know who is in close contact with this Picasso man to leave this quarter as soon as possible for military involvement to happen soon." He leaned in closer to the artist and whispered, "There is a caravan of people a few blocks away from here. Midnight at the north tower, a man named Germel will lead them for America; if you still wish to see the end of this war, go there."

"America?" Picasso said aloud.

"What about America?" The older soldier stood up firmly and addressed the artist as a seasoned soldier. "The North American country is the land of supposed freedom, but we all know that it is full of sub humans and capitalists. A lifestyle that the Third Reich will not stand for from their allies, their enemies, or the world."

Picasso understood what he was to do. The soldier started to leave and took a second to see the *Guernica that* his peer had mistakenly thought was his own. He had heard of the piece before, and he couldn't imagine ever seeing the masterpiece in real life. The artist, seeing that the soldier was preoccupied, spoke up, "I drew this painting for you."

He put his head down. "I know. I'm sorry we didn't listen."

"Don't be sorry to me. Be sorry to those you never warned."

Picasso left for America later that night and continued to make works of a genius that still inspires those around the globe. His art is a reminder of what human ingenuity and greatness can give so many of us. The older Nazi soldier died later that week while in battle, and according to his eulogy written by the Nazi army, he died for the greatness of the Fuhrer and the regime. No mention of the art studio was ever discussed by anyone.

Words on a Cup

Words on a Cup

The other day, I went to the mall in search of a particular item. Now, I am not one who enjoys shopping, like many that I see with bags and bags of goodies, some of which they need and most of which they want; when I can, I order online items of questionable necessity in my life and allow the order to arrive at my house a few days later, but I had to go to the bank to get some cash and thought that going to the mall would not be too far out of my way. Like many things in life, my decision was based on convenience more than anything else. Don't underestimate how much convenience can dictate your decisions. Even the important decisions come down to it, even though we are all told otherwise.

For some time, I have been searching for a picture of Shakespeare. Not the one taken during his lifetime, but the world-famous picture of the man, the image on the First Folio cover that many come to identify the playwright. The journey to obtain the portrait of a man who many can name as easily as their own friends is harder than one would think as there are many images of the man, and many even claim to be him, but there are only a few that are authentic. (I am talking of William Shakespeare here, as I did not mention his entire name, as I am sure that the audience knows only one man with that last name) Regarding the trueness of the portraits, I only wanted one image of the man, not one of when he was 24 or one that someone took as a memory. I wanted the one certain image of the guy, which I am sure did not make my search any easier. There are those who claim that the man didn't even exist, and here I am, trying to get a very specific image of the guy.

My reason for desiring such an item is because of stories I learned of many past writers who had Shakespeare nearby for inspiration. I do not recall any names in particular (for there are too many to count), but I can say for certain there was one writer who had a bust of Shakespeare by his desk for whenever a thought popped into his head. Another had all of the man's plays and works right by his side when writing. One, I believe, even memorized all of the words of the famous writer. Every single word. The guy read Shakespeare so much that he knew everything the English writer ever wrote. That is dedication that I cannot claim towards the career of the poet. As a writer, I can agree with the sentiment that the appearance of Shakespeare makes you strive to be better as a wordsmith, to be more sophisticated than usual, and to edit that phrase a little neater, all because of the mythic stature that Shakespeare has engulfed in our society. To a commonplace author with no audience or publication history, Shakespeare is equivalent to a god. His renown and popularity are something writers only dream of but know they can never truly attain. Before learning Shakespeare, you could never truly grasp what words can do to the world or what the written language can give to fellow men. Because of The Bard, the words can very well be mightier than the sword. Words become thought, and thought becomes action. You feel a certain pressure to compete with Shakespeare when that book of his sits by your desk, to give Romeo a run for his money, to try to write a quote that Hamlet would be proud of, even though most would agree that is not happening anytime soon. Sorry, I'm sure your manuscript is great and all; I personally loved how you didn't start the action of the plot until the second act, but we are talking about the best of the best here, not another published author who is happy to have their book in a library. Unless you have a better line than *To be or not to be* and you have been hiding it away in one of your notebooks for none of us to see, which is really quite a selfish act for you to do, then I wouldn't get your hopes up there, buddy. Greatness should be shared with the world to inspire them to reach such standards in their own life.

That actually reminds me of the one time I once saw an interview with a few older actors, Mel Gibson and Donald Glover, about their *Lethal Weapon* movies and how they have become the epitome of buddy cop movies since the thirty years since they first arrived in cinema. During the interview, Glover was asked about his signature line, "I am getting too old for this shit." and how it feels to have the *To be or not to be* of that genre, which got me thinking about what genre is *To be or not to be* if it is used as the general phrase to describe a standout line. That is how influential Shakespeare has become; his phrases are placements not for any words but for the best of their kind.

I often hear men and women mock a person for trying to sound poetic but failing miserably if a musician rhymes words that are all too obvious to the listener or if a marketer comes up with a silly pun to sell a product. One person in the room will comment, saying, "Watch out. We got William Shakespeare over here." The joke is very clear. Shakespeare could write. You cannot. Even the mind of the average reader, one that is not that much to write about, to begin with, can notice that. Why a bust or a picture of the guy will make me reach that immortal status is something nobody really knows. Like a baseball player with their superstitions. Does putting your clothes on in a certain order really help you pitch better? Does eating a turkey sandwich before every game really help you hit home runs? Probably not. But if you feel it does, then what is the harm in it?

Once I learned of the writers of the past going to Shakespeare for inspiration, I naturally looked around my own office to see if I had anything of the man. To my surprise, I did not. Sure, I have a book of his complete works, but that is on a bookshelf in another room. I have nothing that I look at like those writers did of that bust. I have a few sports signs, a few classic album covers, and a few taped papers that are supposed to be reminders. Somehow, while composing the room, I never thought of making space for a picture of Shakespeare. Luckily, right by the door, there are a few inches for another picture.

One of the biggest pain in the butt when I go to a public place, one with plenty of cars and even more parking spots, is where the hell I am going to park the car. When I was in college, I made it a point to park in the same spot every time, or at least in the same area of the college, so I always knew where the car was. This helped me on some days when the classes were close to that one parking lot, and bad on other days when it was not by the parking lot, and I had to walk across campus. There were a few times when I would walk across campus and see multiple open spots in other parking lots, closer to the building that I was walking into, but I still stuck to the theory of parking in one spot, which I know is better than not. Some of the girls that I knew then were not that crazy about this idea, especially when I had to drive the girl home. That is another tale for another day, though.

Nobody was in the mall when I first walked in. Sometimes, as I enter, a stranger exits the mall, and I am left with the split-second decision of whether to hold the door for them or not. You may say that this thought is pointless to have and that I am better off holding the door without hesitation. What kind of animal am I that I don't even want to hold a door for another, to be more fascinated with myself than others? A human, I believe that is what call ourselves, unless you are Mark Zuckerberg and have a hard time even admitting that. Did we change our identity, and no one told me? Anxiety builds in me as I see a person leaving and as I am going because I believe goodness is contagious. Yes, like that cold you got last week, goodness can be spread from person to person without any sneezing, too. How many times have you said hello to a stranger not because you actually care for them but because someone moments ago said hi to you? My door-holding can lead to someone else holding a door, which could lead to another good deed and so forth, and so forth, until someone discovers the cure for cancer, and people want to know who is to blame. I will gladly take recognition. If I hadn't done my good deed, then the domino effect would have stopped. What is terrifying about this process is that I have cured cancer and been a mass murderer in my lifetime because of it. In a matter of a few seconds, that meeting with a complete stranger is the most important the world has ever seen. Of course, no one notices it, and we all only talk about politicians and wars and laws as the key to change. Convenience and the spreading of vibes, or whatever you want to call those things, are really unspoken matters in our world, and they don't get talked about.

Having said all of that, I did not have to decide on whether I was to hold the door open for someone or not. I know, right, the tragedy of our times.

On a summer day when the humidity can suffocate you and the heat melts your skin, the AC of the mall delightfully hits you and allows those jeans shorts or that tube top you are wearing to fit a little bit better. You are letting out more water than a dam, which I find makes my days much more pleasant. Oddly enough, this destination, one known for its retail stores that all seem to sell the same thing but have enough distinction that they need their own store, has become a hotspot for early morning walkers, for those who wish to avoid the sun's rays, and I must say I agree with this idea. I have seen many walkers and runners in various degrees, from a fifty-degree early morning jog around the neighborhood to a one-hundred-degree noon sunny day jog at the local track, and the one where I am leisurely strolling in a cool facility easily takes the cake. I would like to think that one person accidentally stumbled upon this idea when they were stuck walking in the mall one day, like a lightbulb just went off in their head, "I have feet, and the mall provides a path for me. The path inside is better than the heat outside. Oh my god! I can walk inside! Why have I never thought of this before!"

The person then tells the next fifteen people that they meet that they came up with this great idea, walking inside the mall like we are all supposed to celebrate it. The world is too busy for that sort of stuff, as we all need to get back to the jobs that under-pay us or to eat the food that is determined to kill us, either through starving us as we can't afford it or poisoning us with the crap the companies put in them. Sure, the morning mall walk may become a trend in the local community, and there may even be a funny, bright t-shirt that is made up with a witty slogan like, *Morning mall walker, make way!* But that does not mean the world has time for it. What is really funny is that of the fifteen people the innovator of the mall walking talked to, you know that one of them would eventually wear a silly t-shirt promoting their interest in the hobby as if they didn't ignore the innovator when first presented with the proposal.

As soon as you walk into the mall, you will see an arcade that doesn't know what it wants to be. When I say that it is an arcade, I also mean it is a bar, and a bowling alley, and a party game place. Yeah, the people who owned the place just threw whatever the hell they could together in one space. The notable thing about the place, aside from the obvious identity crisis it is having, is the two crowds it holds in certain areas. First are the people who play the game Dance Dance Revolution professionally or as though there is money in it. The guy, who is about the same fitness level as me, which is saying zero, has knee pads on to play the game. For those who do not know the objective of the game, you must put your feet on the floor panel as the corresponding notes display on the screen. There are guys who spend hours each day playing this game. It is the one thing that you are bound to see when you go into the arcade/bar/bowling alley. The other spot that you may notice is the place with all the arcades for Asian people. I can say that confidently because the games are in Korean, Japanese, or one of the Asian languages. It definitely was not Italian. The room has about twenty fighting arcade games, and I guess they use it for tournaments. I had yet to see any tournaments when I was there.

I once went on a date with a girl I met online at the arcade/bar/bowling alley. It was not a bad time, but I was more into her than she was me. Her name was Bridgette. We went over to the bar and had some drinks and played a round of bowling. She enjoyed herself, but she didn't call me back or anything. My guess is that she was more into the Dance Dance, or Asian fighting game crowd.

After passing the place of the professional dancers, Asian gamers, and a lost date, I walked by a few stores and headed into a variety store, one that sold the type of stuff that you would see at a yard sale. These people are selling that crap all the time. The funky kind of stuff that is cute when you have one of them, but too many of them can be seen as tacky. You know what I am talking about, like a mini-piano that lights up or a fish on a hook that when you pull it, the fish goes back in the water. Someone definitely needs to tell this store that moderation is a thing. I felt that would be my best bet to find the Shakespeare picture. I mean, if you can't get a picture of the Bard while you are searching for funny trinkets like a pink ball that, when it gets wet, becomes red, or an oversized coffee mug with a quote from The Office, then where can you find it?

Across the other side of the room was a young, attractive Indian girl leaning against the glass counter on her phone. She worked there; at least, that is what she tells others when she is asked about her occupation. She doesn't actually work there; she is merely there during the hours she gets paid. Despite the pretty co-worker being the nicest thing I would see that day, I avoided contact with her and any other employee, for I heard from a friend that the employees are trained to ask if you need something every fifteen seconds, every ten seconds if you are standing still.

I walked over to the wall that had all sorts of figures. My god, one for every kind of everything for every person you ever know. If you need to buy a gift for someone, you can go to this part of the store and literally reach out, grab something, and then hand it over as a gift. Later on, you may have to explain to your cousin why you thought getting him a statue of Minnie Mouse was a good idea.

I don't understand how we can have only two political parties, the donkeys and the elephants, but I can go to a store and buy ten different kinds of Batman figures. Who knew that there is less sophistication in politics than in figure-making? That makes sense, I guess; politics only makes laws, business makes money, and man will always come up with another reason for another dollar to be made. Although there is a part of me that is worried that business is getting that much attention as compared to the things that control how we live. But I digress...

I picked up a white cup on the shelf. It was not an ordinary cup like you would drink juices from, nor was it one of those red plastic cups that kids use to drink, but a simple, bland white coffee cup. Nothing about it at first caught my eye. How could it? I have seen hundreds of coffee cups in my life with the same composition as this one. That was only because the picture of a famous American author was turned facing the wall. As I turned the cup around, I exposed a picture of Edgar Allan Poe with the words *Cool Story Poe* in large black capitalized letters. The picture of the poet is the one we have all come to identify him as well. The phrase is, of course, a play on words for *Cool Story Bro.* I personally distrust any individual who compliments my story before I tell it. They either know I am a great storyteller, in which case, they should wait for me to at least tell the story before praising it. That is like laughing at a joke that you heard once before because you know the punchline. Please have some courtesy and laugh when it is appropriate. Or the person with the phrase is mocking me and my art of storytelling. (They wouldn't be the first ones to do that.) Most would not find this offensive, but as a man who tells stories, to be told in a sarcastic manner by a complete stranger before we meet that, my stories stink is too much for me. This is the origin of the phrase that is on a cup for one of the greatest writers of all time. The guy wrote *The Raven*, invented the murder mystery genre, and helped define the macabre genre, and all they could come up with was a phrase for rude people and jokesters.

Some literary minds must have thought it would be cute to include one of literature's most famous writers with the slang term. I would like to imagine the scene played out as follows, "You know Poe rhymes with Bro."

"Yeah, so." The other person at the table would answer.

"We should put *Cool Story Poe* on one of our cups."

"Didn't that guy write stuff that is like, you know, classic?"

"That is not important."

Then, the person who first started walking inside the mall enters the scene and notifies them of this brand-new idea: walking inside the mall.

How the makers of the cup pass upon the words of a man for a more modern phrase is something I don't get. Is Poe's catalog not big enough for people to pick a few words from them? Poems, short stories, a novel, my god, I believe the man was a notable literary critic in his day, too. None of those words are worthy of being on a cup with the man's face. I find that hard to figure. And I am not even a baseball player. Perhaps I would be better off if I did put my clothes on in a certain order.

I have seen stuff like that done before in an attempt by the sellers to appeal to the youth. Abraham Lincoln wearing sunglasses, George Washington riding a dragon, because our traditional view of these men is not very interesting to the young ones today. The one guy created a nation where the life of a man is built on his character, not heritage, and the other saved that nation from destruction. Do people who wear sunglasses and like dragons not like freedom as it is? Is the story of our nation's history not interesting enough for them? Well, excuse me; I didn't know they needed style to attract you to it. I am reminded of a comment by a fellow writer when he spoke of his inspiration at a book conference. Now, you may expect him to give the normal answer of Shakespeare and other classic writers that we all know. Perhaps a few takes on their stories and a mention of one or two obscure writers, but he did not. Instead, he spoke of how books like *To Kill A Mocking Bird* did not appeal to him and how that work did not speak to him. The message of respect for others and not judging a man by his looks does not reach everyone, I suppose. What does it say about literature if some in it, do not understand the past? I will let you decide that answer for yourself.

I did not find any picture of Shakespeare and left the store shortly after.

There was something unnatural about that cup, though, that I could not stop thinking about since seeing it.

There is something wrong with it. Is it? To write these words and put them on a cup, a t-shirt, a sticker, a phone case, a bag, and anything in between. These can become one of those objects just as easily as they can be read. A poster on your wall, a note on your desktop, a trinket that turns different colors, or a mini figure that has ten different varieties.

Is this popularity noteworthy? To be celebrated with a party and alcohol. Please fetch me a drink for this great accomplishment. I will be like an Irishman and drink until I cannot anymore. I believe that is just another day for an Irishman, but regardless my stand stays still that the growth of these words deserves a drink.

Or is it a sham to my very words, a scheme by a crook, a silent passing to go unnoticed? Will I be caught in a twisted crime to be brought in by the officials? It wasn't me, sir. It was the one-armed man. Please recall when I was brought in as a criminal, the law was interpreted against me. That blood is not mine. I was framed. The judge is in on it. The lawyers, the jury, they are all against me. Remember how quickly the words can be changed when spoken in a courtroom. They have conspired against me to be brought like an evil dictator who abandons his people or a corrupt businessman who buys out all the competition. All for words on a cup.

There is a disturbing force out in the world that I do not trust. It can shape how you view the very words on this page, that one line that moved you, that one excerpt that you remember for a later date. It can take any line here and put it on a product and sell it. That's not normal. I can't put my finger on it, but when I go to the movies to see a film, then to a fast food place to eat and see the face of the woman in the film on a cup with my meal and then go to the store and see that same woman's face on products on products like t-shirts and bookbags and anything else that a consumer will mindlessly buy. My financial mind says it is capitalism, but my rational mind says it is more than that. There is no free enterprise with that system, only a controlled enterprise. Bear in mind that I have very little money in my name, and I am a writer, so my thinking may not be entirely sound.

I headed back towards the entrance and noted that there was not a single person on that dancing game, and I saw a few Asians by the arcade. I noted the drink that I had with that Bridgette girl, who thought that she was a 10, as many girls today think they are, but was no more than a 6. My drink was a Margherita, but the flavor was blueberry. Yeah, and the girl got a drink like that, too!

I took one last look at the arcade, remembering that I did want to go to the park for a date instead.

"We should have just walked around the mall," I said aloud.

As I headed toward the exit, an older woman came by, and I held the door open for her. In a few years, I may have solved world hunger, made a few vital laws, and started the next world war, all from that very moment of holding the door open for the stranger.

I drove home not caring about my search for the picture of the poet anymore. What was really gained from it? What is the difference between the picture in my room or not?

As I parked the car, I headed inside. "Damn," I said as I opened the door. "I forgot to go to the bank."

Not Too Late

Not Too Late

Sean sat in the slightly reclined passenger seat of his ten year old Nissan that needed new brakes he couldn't afford, as he waited for the last customer to arrive at the market on the hot humid afternoon. Reigel. Phil Reigel is his name. He ordered yellow string beans that weigh out to 1.07 lb., chick peas, an eight pack of frozen patties that weigh out to 4.445 lb. and a chicken garlic sausage that expires within the next week.

Once Sean completed the setup of the market, which included putting the gray table, medium cooler, and brown bags behind his car and a light blue sign with the company's logo, *Your Foods*, on his windshield, he pulled out his book of complete short stories of Ernest Hemingway, and read to pass the time. The medium cooler held the food that was to be kept cold during the two-hour window. The brown bags had the pantry items already in them, and the gray table was where the brown bags stayed to be picked up by the customers. The book, which was not going to be picked up by any customer, was a La Vigia edition of the short stories by the classic author since it was not compiled by him but by his sons. The edition's name is a take on the place where the author spent his last days in comfort and solemn.

Reigel's order was not enough to truly frustrate the one-year employee of the online marketplace, for it had a quantity that looked like a customer put some thought and time into their selection, unlike some customers who order only a two-pound salmon and never pick it up. This is wasted time in Sean's eyes, for he could be spending his time on his career rather than sitting in the parking lot of a catholic school to give food to people too lazy to go to the grocery store themselves. Do not ask Sean if this action is a waste in his eyes, though, for he may have a wiseass remark that draws you away from his otherwise laidback, relaxed demeanor. "This job is a waste of time." He might say. Sean is what you may call a charming fellow.

It is always nice to hear about the usage of time and the effectiveness of it by those who seem only good at avoiding the very topic. You never ask a busy person about the time, for they have things to do (and have ordered their food to be picked up at a local catholic school). The only person who ever has an opinion on time are those that waste it.

The chickpeas, which up until recently Sean did not know were used to make hummus, and the yellow string beans, which Sean is fairly certain are not used in any hummus, were in double-bagged brown bags labeled with black marker ink for Riegel. The patties and sausage were wrapped in separate butcher paper, and at the bottom of the cooler, they were filled with ice.

Sean was reading a story of a boxer with insomnia. The guy will lose the fight based on his lack of sleep more than anything. This kind of story that centers around boxing is a good chance of pace for Sean as a reader since the last few he read by Hemingway had to do with bullfighting, which bored him after a while. Sean knows nothing of the sport, unlike boxing, which he does not follow as a fan would, but he does know enough that he can understand it. He knows the often-quoted comment, "Why is a boxing ring a square?" which it should be noted is never remarked by boxing fans. It is like when comedians give their takes on the Catholic Church; you are unsure if you are to take them seriously since their expertise in the subject is limited. Plus, you are drunk (at least I am when I go to comedy clubs). Sean can also tell you that Muhammad Ali's name was Cassius Clay when he won the gold medal, and before he went all rejection of society while being the center of attention. There was always a level of fakeness to Ali that Sean didn't care much for. The guy literally fights for a living; he goes into a ring (or square if you want to be technical), punches a guy to a pulp, and then a victor is decided, but going overseas and dying for your nation is too much for him. Ali was tough enough to take punches but not enough to face death. Then Sean hears many talks of how Ali stood up for what he believed in, which makes Sean wonder if the average person, who is not Muslim and can tell you nothing about the Quaran, knows that part of Ali's beliefs was being Muslim and reading the Quran. This is not even bringing up that there is a theory in the boxing community that Frazier threw the fight against Ali, as many are not sure how a punch as weak as the one that Ali threw could knock down a fighter like Frazier. Don't believe me? Watch the video yourself and notice how Ali's seemingly regular punch knocked out his opponent. Sean could tell you about this all, but not bullfighting. There is not a single person that Sean ever met in his life that knows anything about the sport. If it had not been for Hemingway to write about it so much, Sean would have had zero information on it.

The worker, who is not doing much work, has noticed that insomnia is an odd theme in a few of Hemingway's works, and he has wondered while reading the compilation if the writer had it. If an author speaks of a certain theme enough, that means that the very theme is a part of the author's life, right? Then again, Sean doesn't get too far with all that, as he learned once about doctors evaluating characters from *Seinfeld*, the TV show, and giving them medical disorders. There are people out there who are watching a comedy and wondering what they can take away from it for their medical career. It seems those in the food industry aren't the only ones not working.

If you were to take your food from Sean, you would not get any opinion on Muhammad Ali, Hemingway, or Seinfeld, only a simple statement of "Here you go" with the bags. Opinions are only good for those who want to hear it, and people coming to a place to get their groceries are not those people. Also, Sean is not the friendliest of people, as even his normal remarks come across as wiseass insults. Despite all the reading the guy does, Sean has learned how to treat his fellow man with common decency.

Every car that comes by in the parking lot of the Catholic school catches Sean's attention and causes him to pick his face from the book. Each car is the potential that he sees his last customer, which means his night is over. It was only five minutes ago that the parking lot was filled with large yellow school buses for the summer camp being held there. Sean does not know of the camp nor has any interest in it; besides, its effect on his own work is minimal. Many children left the school and entered the buses, backpacks in hand and summertime excitement still in their hearts.

Behind his car is a carnival in town. A carnival, up until parking by it, Sean did not know existed. The carnival had the setup that any who has attended the event knows of rigged machines waiting for the one sucker to spend hundreds of dollars trying to win, unhealthy food that no one in their right mind would eat if not at the carnival, bright lights on anything nailed down, and rides that are enough to be fun, but can also be potentially dangerous. Carnivals are casinos for kids, in that no matter how much you want to avoid going, you are going to go there to see what is going on. (You may be able to beat that one game this year. They may have the fried Oreos that you love so much. The bright lights are not that distracting; they are even charming when you view them in the dark. And the rides are not that bad. How many people have died while going on them? I rest my case). Sean did not give too much attention to the carnival and its rides. For the reader's sake, that may be best.

In front of his car, about twenty feet away on the sidewalk that connects to the school, were two workers by a cart moving whatever packages they were instructed to by their job responsibilities. One was a twenty-five-year-old who got the job of cleaning up the school during the summer through his uncle, who was a teacher there during the school year. The other was a forty-five-year-old bald man who had been working there since he was twenty. Both had the look on their face that maintenance workers have when they realize that they are stuck doing tasks that they would rather not do, such as cleaning a toilet or taking out the trash. Neither wanted to do it, but both knew they had to and accepted their reality. Part of their acceptance is getting the work done at their own speed and not killing themselves over it. Moving the carts to the other building in the middle of the afternoon was part of it. They did all that they were supposed to, but that is it. Giving more when nothing is expected is stupid in the eyes of a janitor.

Sean stared at them for a brief second as the book sat in his lap. Neither seemed to even know or care what was in the packages that were clearly too large for them to carry. He continued to stare until they got to the side entrance to the school. The old man opened the door first, and the younger man pushed the cart with the packages. For a moment, it appeared that the packages would fall over, but the young man stopped himself, repositioned the packages on the center of the cart, and pushed it forward as the old man pulled it through the door. They turned quickly right down the hallway of the school out of Sean's sight.

Before continuing the story Sean got struck with a question of the author. "Why does everyone in a Hemingway story add water to liquor? Do people really do that?" He has no answer for this. He would not address a customer about this inquiry either. Sean failed to see that the drinking habits of authors in the past were simply different than those of his time.

For two hours, the customers of the online marketplace who placed an order of their food on the site have to go to the pickup site to get their order. This particular day, Sean chose to drive his own car to the market, rather than the company car, because the market is right down the block from his home, and he will leave work right afterward, rather than having to drive back to the office and then drive home from there. Because the market is from 4 to 6, Sean can leave earlier than six if all the customers show up before then. The latest he can leave is six, and at that point, he will call the customer, using the number on the customer order sheet and his phone, and inform the late customer that the market is closed and that they can pick up their food at a later time.

Today went pretty well so far for Sean; by that, I mean he will get out early, not that his performance is outstanding, for handing bags of food to strangers is neither a mentally strenuous nor physically exhausting job. The first customer, Katie U, picked up the order at 4:05 PM. It consisted of two whole gallons of milk, one pound of tuna, one pound of salmon, fuji apples, Winesap apples, and Honeycrisp apples (all 2.5 lb each). Although the name on the order for Katie U was that of a female, a man of 30 years of age, in flip-flops and starting to gray around his beard, showed up to pick up the order instead. The man, who appeared to only listen to heavy metal and yet was very chill in his demeanor, quickly told Sean that he was there to pick up Katie U's order.

"Katie U?" Sean confirmed. And away went all the bags for that customer.

Sean didn't even have any time to think about the woman's last name before another customer showed up. The second customer, Priscilla Castina, picked up her order at 4:10 PM. Hers was not nearly as large as U's, only containing three fat-free milks, two edamame dips, broccoli, and organic carrots. She was a 50-year-old woman no bigger than many of the bags. It is not out of line to say that the order weighed more than the woman, who seemed to be much older than her already old appearance. She was neither kind nor forceful with Sean, only a matter of fact. She wanted her food, and Sean had it. Of course, she was in no position to do much if Sean was to reject that offer, but there is no good that would come from such behavior. Sean wanted her to leave, and she wanted to get out of there as soon as possible.

After emptying out the two customers that arrived within the first 15 minutes of the time, Sean was optimistic that this would actually be an easy day, and that he can then get some stuff done later on.

"Great. Now, all I need is for one customer to show up." Sean checked the name "Reigel."

By the curb of the carnival were two African American men dressed in the same attire as the one who worked for the carnival. One was tall and skinny and new to the job and got it as his other job, as a security guard, didn't work. The other, who is much older than him, has more white hair on his face than black skin, had been there all of his life, and the carnival is all he knows.

"You hear that?" The younger of the two asked. He was referring to the sound on one of the rides that they stood by. If one didn't know any better, you would have thought the machine was breaking.

"I don't play with that when I am working. Yo son, I'm working. That ain't gonna happen. Never did happen, never gonna happen." The older of the two spoke, facing away from the other. He finished his proclamation of caution as he lit his joint. "You motherfucker want to fool around. That ain't happening on my watch. Nope. Not me."

"Damn, nigga, what are you gonna do about it?" The younger of the two responded, upset at the indifference his senior co-worker had about a situation he felt could cost the life of a carnival customer.

He spoke to the other with the n-word as though it was not an insult and something that he only said when he knew that it was appropriate. Now was one of those times.

"Listen, listen listen." The older worker put his hand on the shoulder of the younger. The senior was tall enough that the stretch of his hand didn't make the exchange awkward for him, as though he has done this many times before. "I am going to take care of it."

"By leaving?"

He took his hand off the youth's shoulder and turned away from him. He didn't say anything and finished smoking his joint. "It's fine. It's fine." The older of the two kept repeating as he smoked his joint.

The younger carnival worker walked away disgruntled.

An African American girl who was about the same age as the younger one (both in their early twenties), also dressed up as though she worked for the carnival, went up to the older worker. She was not in the mood to confront either of her co-workers only to get done with her shift.

Unfortunately, she knew there was no way of avoiding either of them.

The older worker addressed her, "It's fine. It always sounds like that. It's fine."

He took one last puff, and then the two walked back out of sight of Sean and the food.

Sean didn't address either of the carnival workers or their conversation, as he was more interested in his own job and the last customer showing up. Only for a split second did the food vendor think that if anything happened at the carnival to the one ride, then one of the guys who was talking might be accountable. Like I said, though, this didn't interest him.

Sean wasn't even interested in the use of the n-word by the African American men and how that is only acceptable when the word is used as an address by friends, similar to dude or bro. White people don't understand this, and when they use the n-word, they are saying it in a disparaging way, not as a neutral address towards an acquaintance. The backstory and current use of one of the most controversial words of our time was not on the mind of the food vendor.

Having no more interesting things going around him, as the buses with the schoolkids were gone, the janitors with their packages left, and the carnival workers arguing were no where in sight, Sean took a nap to pass the time. If the customer is here when he is sleeping, then the person will simply have to wake him up. That was the philosophy that Sean had.

He dozed off for some time, and once awake from his nap, he got up from his seat and walked towards the exit of the parking lot to see if a car was coming. It wasn't. I am not sure why the man thought that walking towards the exit at that exact time would help him, and once he took a few steps towards it, he went back towards his car.

He checked the brown bags on the table, to make sure they didn't fall over, as that has happened one too many times in his food market days. Sean would leave the bags out on the table and then when the customer showed up, the food would be all over the ground, as the wind knocked over the bag. That did not happen today, as the summer heat was more prevalent than the wind.

Sean then finished reading what he could of his Hemingway stories (the fighter lost the fight), but even then, every five minutes, he kept looking at his watch, hoping that the customer would come. By the time it got to 5:30, the prospect of leaving early was gone. He started at 4 PM and ended at 6 PM; if he left at 5:30, he was not leaving early at all.

When the stories didn't fascinate him much longer, he looked at the three sheets of orders that he had for the day. Two of them were already gone, and the sheets were marked with the time the customer showed up. He only had one sheet that was not marked off. Reigel.

One stranger was the difference between Sean leaving an hour and a half earlier at his job. Of course, the stranger did not know that.

Time went, and went and went. And Sean continued to sit there tired of waiting, but also aware that he had no other choice than to wait. He wasn't even interested in the short stories anymore, as all he wanted to do was leave, but that could not happen is there was no customer named Reigel to pick up that last bag.

Were there other things that Sean could have thought about? Surely, he could have addressed the very nature of the fight in the short story he read. The fighter lost the fight but also bet on himself to lose, so he did win, in a way. There is a philosophical question the story grips about winning and losing.

Sean could have thought about how he heard the current Catholic school his car was parked in was closing. Just a few weeks ago, the school sent out a notice to the parents and the kids that the school would no longer be around. Where will the Catholics go when there are no more Catholic schools? Public schools, I guess.

If Sean was really feeling frisky with his wandering mind, he could think about how his Catholic beliefs led him to one conclusion about the classic author who wrote too much about bullfighting. The guy is in Hell, for those who commit the act of suicide have given up on God and are, therefore, going to Hell. Or something like that. (Pardon my lack of knowledge on this topic. I didn't go to Catholic school) Perhaps Sean can better explain than me. But according to the Church, one of the greatest writers of all time is suffering in Hell for ending his own life.

And did Sean take any of his time to think about any of these things? Of course he didn't. He has better things to do. What those things are is something I don't even know, but something tells me they are not as alluring as Sean makes them out to be.

At 5:55 PM, just as Sean was about to get ready to pack up, he saw a car drive fast into the parking lot, not even parking properly in a space. Out ran a 35-year-old Asian man with sunglasses on, jean shorts, and a blue shirt, "Hey man. Sorry, I am late. I am here to pick up the food my wife ordered."

"Reigel."

" That is her."

Sean took the frozen food out of the cooler and put it in the brown bag, handing over the bag without any wiseass comments or anything controversial to say.

"This is it?" The customer handled the bags surprised at the presentation of it all, for normally it was his wife picking up the food.

"Sorry for being so late. I got stuck in traffic, and I did the best I could to get here. I got off of one exit only to get into traffic at the other. My wife is working late tonight, and I am stuck doing the grocery duties."

"Okay, have a nice night," Sean said in a stale tone.

"Thanks, man. This all looks great." He took one more second to look at the stuff in the bag. "Enjoy the rest of your evening." Mr. Reigel left with his bags and drove off.

Sean packed up his stuff and got out of there as soon as he could. He threw the table in the trunk, not caring about its placement and whether it would move as he drove. He then stuffed the cooler in his back seat, a tough fit for his car but one that could work, especially now that the cooler was empty. When he was all done, he looked at the time in his car. It read 6:01 PM. "It is good to know that I didn't completely waste my time." He said aloud.

Sean drove after the shift ended.

Leapfrog

Leapfrog

As an older man filled with more wisdom and knowledge than my youth due to my years of living more than any attempt of enlightenment on my part, I can still remember a line one of my teachers from eighth grade said, not of with any true knowledge or wisdom, but for its timeless humor. His remark was of a compromised sexual position picture of two rhinoceros.

I'm sure there are some readers out there who find quotes in more traditional formats like that of The Bible with its parables on love and God or the classic writers like Wilde and Twain, whose wit still makes us chuckle at their offbeat truthfulness. I myself have just finished the book *Tender Is The Night* by the classic writer F. Scott Fitzgerald; it is about a doctor married to a schizophrenic and how he copes with his alcoholism and infidelity. In the book, between the French lines that made it difficult for a foreigner of that language to read and Fitzgerald's poetic verse that runs smoother than the rivers, the words fit more for an Ancient Eastern philosophy book, "Do not let the loss of a battle lead you to think that you lost the war." How great a line to utter to a friend as we walk along the channels of life approached by obstacles and questions at every turn. That was not the quote from my teacher.

On the presentation screen at the front of the room was a clip being played of the natural environment, one I am sure you have seen or at least familiar with, for I feel the schools have been playing the same five videos of animals in the wild for the past 50 years. (That or all videos of animals appear the same to me because they are doing nothing more than sitting there eating grass) The video shows animals at their primal best, without humans, and reacting to their most basic instincts of survival and nurture. A lion kills the one antelope who is lost from the herd and cannot fight against the king of the jungle. A pack of ants carry tiny bits of dirt to the top of the anthill, more organized than most of humanity's greatest teams. A panther, in its mysterious pose, stares off from the mountaintop. The narrator has a dull, bland voice with no inflection and so little interest you could have sworn he was trying to be that way. Each scene of the animal on the frame is only a few seconds long for the viewer to appreciate nature, but not enough to learn anything of substance from it. By the time you identify the animal on screen, they are on another animal in another part of the world. There, for a whole minute, appeared in the African desert two large animals in a position not for four-legged creatures.

The teacher of the class, Mr. Potto, was standing by the screen as this image popped up and did his best to salvage what he could of the innocence many of us had all but rid of from overexposure to visual media.

"They are just playing Leapfrog, kiddies. That's all. Leapfrog." Mr. Potto said to the young audience, confronting the reality that none of us got his humor. We knew it was dirty. We knew it was bad. We knew it was sex, but as to why he would use the term leapfrog was a lesson we were all too young for.

In this class of only the A students, aka smart kids, we were supposed to learn of the environment, of rocks and decay, earth and rubble, and all the grounds and sky we live in. I, in my wasteful youth, did very little of that. All I can truthfully tell you is some minor anecdotes from that time that may not be considered worth reading or remembering for a stranger, but for me, they are as a part of my life as the morning's breakfast. I sat next to a kid in the middle of the classroom who was lazier than me in Matt Constant. He was the type of kid who could have gone on to a prestigious college in engineering and done very well for himself by inventing a machine or equation or another innovation that many would marvel at with wonder. Unfortunately, he did not do any of this, far from it, for drugs, notably weed, and cigarettes, and the financial demands of life got the best of him, and as you see him working at a fast food place, you would have no clue that the man was once thought of by his peers as the smartest and brightest and the one who could change the concrete world. Like many I know, this man did not live up to his potential that once captured his youthful days and now must live with the current reality where he is seen as nothing more than an average worker making minimum wage in a job that requires little thinking from his fast brain. I have to admit that the closeness I have to this man was not what I make it seem to be. I was not his best friend, barely even his friend outside of the one class I sat next to him in. By the time I went off to college, in a position slightly better than my counterpart but by no means great, Matt allowed drugs and beer to wipe away any form of intelligence he had when I sat next to him, astonished that I knew a person that smart. His face was much older than a high school graduate's, his skin was worn, and exhaustion was the only feeling he knew, for the highs were no longer what they once were, and the anxiety still lingered no matter how many packs of cigarettes one goes through. If you look closely and see through the eyes of the disappointment, you may see the same genius that I sat next to. Although you could argue that that boy left as soon as the drugs arrived.

To Matt, school was easy and not as much of a necessity in life to be someone as much as a forceful controlled process by his elders. He could ace tests without studying or without a care in the world. Often, as the tests were being given back to the students, he would show me his grade, as many students did at the time, out of curiosity about their skill level relative to their classmates, and he received the same grades, 97 to 100, only missing a question or two. Some teachers in my classes would include a difficult extra credit question at the end of the tests to challenge those of us who studied the work rather than play video games all night. These were the only questions Matt ever got wrong. I, on the other hand, did not do as well in the science class due to my disinterest in the subject, for I found labs with their microscopes and other equipment boring, and my inability to stay awake in the class didn't help. I never took notes in my notebook or anywhere, and what I did write with my writing tool were scribbles no master of decoding could understand since I was only getting half of the content anyway. For me, to get a 75 with that amount of minimal effort was acceptable, even though the rest of my classmates all got great grades. I say that Matt was the smartest of the bunch, for he was the only one I saw who did not put much effort into it, yet he still succeeded. There were others in the class who had to give their maximum try to get the same results. One boy, with acne skin too much to count and a voice that broke a window frame, Charles, was a know-it-all and sat in front of me and my genius classmate. Not only did he take notes, he questioned some of Mr. Potto's points on various sections of the current lesson. And then there was Victoria, with her long black hair and pretty smile, who had a few questions after we got our tests back. She even asked about the stuff I knew about. After Mr. Potto explained the answer, she always seemed surprised, as if she had not heard about it before.

Besides these random observations I remember nothing scientific of the environmental science class, chiefly due to the fact that I slept more than I participated in it. I attribute this to my late nights of video games. I was not adept with time management at that age. I simply felt that I could keep going all the time, that there was no need for me to get a good's night rest, ever.

And, of course, I remember the comment made by Mr. Potto on what the two one-horned creatures were doing on the screen.

From what I recall, Mr. Potto was a good man, meaning he had no rudeness or meanness to him. Not once did he raise his voice or yell at any of us, even Charles, for trying to one-up him; even when he brought up to the class about my lackluster grades, he did so in a way that wasn't cruel or vicious. He simply said that some in the class did not do that great and moved on with the lesson. He wanted, as any teacher does, the room of advanced students to like the subject of rocks and volcanoes, but he knew that was not likely. Despite this fact, the presentations we saw in each class show how much he loved his work. Each had elaborate sliding actions for pictures and quotes from pop culture references the kids would understand, all much more than most teachers do. He tried to make us enjoy the material the best way he could. Today, in the same classroom with the same black solid desks with the same two chairs each, sitting by the same radiator by the same window, is my same teacher, playing the same video of the same two rhinoceros in the same dry humor saying the same thing he told my class to a new group of students. To an adolescent kid, that sort of thing is funny, like a dirty joke about a person's name sounding like a body part, like Uranus or Dick, but to me, in my mature years, I would not see it so. For Mr. Potto to see me where I am now would be a surprise and prompt a sarcastic remark about my current state as a writer and that he is a source for it. "Great, the guy who couldn't even stay awake in my class wrote a story about me, and did he include the lessons I taught on science or the planet? No. He wrote about my reaction to two animals having sex. It's nice to know that my words go somewhere." There is an odd sense of irony in that statement. The man who is telling his side of the story, who remembered him, is one who barely participated and one who, it is safe to say, he was disappointed in at the time. How could he not be in me? The rest of the room of twenty students got A's and did not like getting a B. I was the exception in his formulaic teaching that produced results and content with being mediocre in my schoolwork.

I should mention that at the end of the school year, Mr. Potto had an award ceremony where all his students from his science classes, he not only taught the smart students, he taught the regular kids too, would fill the room to hear a presentation for the ones selected by the science teacher. The awards were nothing serious, like that of any other school awards. Mr. Potto took time to give us silly titles like "Most Likely To Never Stop Talking" and "Most Likely To Drop A Microscope." All of us kids were excited to attend such an unusual event on an otherwise boring school day. I arrived late to the meeting because I had to attend detention for another class, but yours truly was not included in any of these awards, from what I know. I could have missed my piece of paper in the early parts of the ceremony, but I doubt it.

Mr. Potto always had a witty line for any situation, like Wilde or other classic writers. He was, and remains, one of the few whose wits outdid my own. If you do see him some time teaching at the old school with his room of students, let him know that I am sorry for sleeping through his class, not that it matters at this point since I am a grown man with other obligations and commitments that deserve my attention and I am sure that my presence in the class has long been forgotten by the man. In hindsight, at my older age, being more fascinated by the world around me for no other reason than my own place in it, I find that stuff that Mr. Potto poured over interesting to learn, and I have taken up a few textbooks on my own to learn some of what I missed. Better than never, I suppose.

I bring up that story in order to tell of another time when the screen of mating animals came to life. Let me explain.

Years after taking the science class, on a night that seemed like any other, meaning that the current state of the New York Yankees and the recent Jeopardy questions occupied everyone's minds, I was hanging out with a friend of mine from school, one that was not in Mr. Potto's class. In the den area of the house where the family watched TV was me, Johnny (my friend from school), and his sister Desiree.

"What do you think the Final Jeopardy question will be about tonight?" Johnny asked us, as he had the most interest in the game. Between the two of us, he follows the show more than me, but I get more answers right than him.

"I don't know, hopefully, something that I know," I responded.

"That is always so hard. I only do well with stuff I know." Desiree commented as the three of us sat there watching TV.

"I hope the Yankees win. They have to be better." My friend said, flipping through the channels of the TV.

"What do you want them to win every game?" I asked my friend.

"What? It can happen."

"I am so hungry. Are either of you hungry?" Desiree said.

"Eh..." We both answered

Just then their mom walked into the room "Hey, I am going to get some pizza, who wants to come with me."

"Johnny said that he would go with you." Desiree volunteered her brother.

"What?"

"Great, Jonathan, I will order two pies for everyone." Being that we were in an Italian-American house, more is always better, as sometime during the weekend, another family member would come into the house and have a slice. We were not going to eat all the ordered pizza and that was part of the plan.

Johnny didn't put up much of a fight and went with his mom to the place down the road. You can still go there as it is in that shopping center by the Chase bank and community park. Although honestly, the pepperoni is not the greatest, and the grandma slices are the only good thing they sell. We only got two pies of regular slices. I was a guest and was not going to be picky about my pizza, not then.

"Hey, me and Mom are going to get the pizza. We will be back in a little bit."

In the room sat me and Desiree, with nothing left to do but watch TV, although our adolescent minds were quick to go other places.

Me and her were left in the room together for quite some time. We were kids at the time, and both had too much energy for our bodies to control, and not enough smarts in our heads to understand it. We were both attracted to each other, in a way that only innocent teenagers could be.

Boys like a girl with big boobs, nice hair, and a fit body, and girls like a guy with a young face, nice hair, and a slim build. If you fit that vague criteria, then the other sex will be attracted to you.

She moved over to me, then me closer to her, until we were next to each other. For a brief moment, we looked at each other like we knew that we got close for a reason.

Both ready to go and eager, and thinking the house was ours, we pounced on each other like a cheetah on prey.

"Now?" I asked, confirming my suspicions, as she grabbed me.

"Stop wasting time. We don't have long." Desiree commanded the more eager of the two.

"What?" I asked, "Are we the only ones home?"

"Oh my god, less talking. The place is 15 minutes away, so you have ten minutes. Hurry up."

After we both got undressed, I tried my best to pin her against the couch, and although I could lift the girl up, she was heavier than she seemed. I won't lie to you and say it was the best and most thrilling, for neither of us knew what we were doing. At one point, I grabbed the wrong hole of hers, and she tugged my private parts too far down. It was awkward as much as it was fun. It is one of those moments that, when I look back on it now, I wonder how we didn't break something in the house, like the TV, or hurt ourselves.

Luckily, about a minute in, she started to tell me what to do while I was on top of her. *Put your hand here. Just like that. No, not that way.* The type of advice that is vague to any not doing the act at the time, but when doing it is the most important thing in the world. Guys never know what to do when having sex, even though it is all we think about.

I finished before her and then got off of her.

"Seriously?" She motioned towards me. "I am not done over here."

"Oh, right." She pushed my head down but then quickly stopped that.

"No, wait. Follow my lead."

She showed me what to do with my fingers for the next few minutes, and she then finished.

For a minute or two we sat there surprised at what just happened, as our clothes were on the floor.

"Did we just do that?" I asked.

"Seems it." She said as she went to the bathroom.

We finished putting our clothes back on before Johnny and his mom returned home with the pizza and acted as though nothing happened cleaning up as best as we could.

"Everyone, we got dinner!" Their mom called out for us to eat.

Johnny and his mother were already at the table as me and Desiree walked over together, trying not to make it appear that a few seconds ago, we were rolling on the ground like two animals. (Two stupid clueless animals, but two animals nevertheless) I thought that I may have left the couch a little off and that someone might guess what happened when

Derick, the younger brother, came from upstairs hollering, "Oh man! I am starving! I am so hungry!"

Johnny answered, "That's because all you do is eat!"

"John, stop that. Derick, sit down and have a slice." Their mom answered.

The family divided the pizza among the sitters, and everyone got what they needed to eat when our attention turned towards the television, which was something Desiree and I were more than happy about. My blood still getting back to its regular flow, and her hair still being fixed.

The local news, which is here in New York, was about a car accident in Canada, which, for those who do not know, is not here in New York.

"Why are they talking about that?" Jonny asked the rest of the table as he faced the television directly.

"It's a tragedy. People died." The mother said, trying to put the accident into some perspective for the pizza eaters.

"Yeah. But that is in Canada. I'm not sure if you noticed but we live in America."

"I hadn't noticed," I commented.

"Why? That is my question. Why? Why include a car accident about a land I will never drive in? They might as well talk about a tragedy from Australia or Saudi Arabia while they are at it."

I stated my opinion. "That's because there weren't enough deaths in America, between all those guns and drugs, so they went to Canada for their campaign to scare everyone."

"It is still sad." The mother somberly mentioned.

"God forbid the news has something nice to say about this land. God knows that it is a battlefield out there, and everyone is trying to kill everyone."

"That's why I don't watch it," Desiree said. "The news is so negative."

That's when her younger brother made a random comment while eating some pepperoni he picked off his slice. "I saw you and Alex playing a game."

We both looked nervously at one another, for we both thought the house was empty and our noise was not heard by anyone. We forgot that her younger brother was asleep in his room upstairs.

Desiree mumbled a response no one heard.

I tried to save the situation and blurted out, "Leapfrog. We were playing Leapfrog."

"Oh." The boy said. "I never saw one played like that before."

"Well, it's a special kind of one." I elaborated. "It's for adults," I whispered to myself.

The child was satisfied with the answer, for the metaphor was over his head, and he had not taken Mr. Potto's class. "Oh, okay."

The other two at the table couldn't believe what they had heard.

"Leapfrog?" Desiree's mother asked.

"Yeah," Desiree confirmed, not missing a beat.

Johnny, the only one at the table who didn't know what was going on and had his eyes on the TV, spoke up. "Why were you two playing leap frog? Leapfrog is a kid's game." I gave him my version of the death stare to stop the conversation, and he got the clue. "Oh... yeah. Leapfrog. Got it."

When I was told about the animals and leapfrog in 8th grade, I thought nothing of it, only a way for my teacher to pass the time. I didn't realize that on a slow night that ended pretty quickly, I would use that excuse as a way to get out of an awkward situation.

The mom and dad of Desiree must have caught on to the metaphor, and I was not invited back over to the house for pizza for a while after that incident. Yeah, apparently, they must have played Leapfrog before, too.

Now, whenever I see a nature documentary that talks about the lions, and the fish and the bears, I only think of one thing; leapfrog, kiddies, they are playing Leapfrog.

Acknowledgements

I want to thank my family for always being there for me in my writing career. You guys always believed in my stories even when I didn't myself, and for that I am grateful.

I also want to thank all the workers from all the jobs that I have had over the years, which is a reflection in this collection. There are so many to count, but if I ever worked with you, then I do thank you for helping me grow as a writer, even though you didn't know it at the time.

I also want to thank God for helping me write these words, as I am not doing this without his help. You guide me when I have nowhere to go, and you give me confidence that my life has meaning. Thank you for that.

These following short stories have all been previously published on the site Pens and Words. Additions have been made to most of them.

- A Trip to the Bookstore
- Mr. Evil and the Tennis Rackets
- The Painting of Paint and Destruction
- The End of Life
- Merchant of Death
- Mask Burning
- Blue Curtain
- No Resolution
- The Gun on the Wall
- Bad Timing at the Ledge

About The Author

Greg Luti is an editor, author, poet and blogger. He runs the literary blog Pens and Words. Everything Must Go is his first short story collection. You can visit his website, gregluti.com for more information about his books.

Further Reading

Keep an eye out for Greg Luti's first novel, The Hit of Henry.

www.ingramcontent.com/pod-product-compliance
Lightning Source LLC
Chambersburg PA
CBHW071425200726
48294CB00002B/522